Forever

Poetic Reflections on Life, Love, Laughter and Loss

Katherine Jones

Forever and Always

Poetic Reflections on Life, Love, Laughter and Loss

© Katherine Jones

Published by Bronwyn Editions via Amazon KDP

Printed by Amazon KDP

in the UK 2024

ISBN: 9798332863530

Cover design by Robert Morris

Contents   Page

Butterflies and Feathers	7
We Did	8
As Goblets Fall to the Ground	10
Effortless	12
Vampires Beware	14
When the Windmills Cease to Turn	16
What Happened to You?	18
The Very Next Station	19
You Can't Argue with a Barcode	21
The Sun That Would Never End	22
Storm Alan	26
The Horizon	28
She Stood on Top of the Cliff and Waited	30
The Fortune Teller's Crystal Ball	32
The Hafod	35
False Toothed Smiles	38
If the Walls had Ears	40
Folded, Crumpled, Creased, or Worn	42
I Once Gave You My Heart	44
Invalid or Invalid?	46
In the Blink of an Eye	48
Strawberries	50
My Love, My Hero	52
When Worlds Collide	55
Those Eyes, Those Lies	59
The Guilt is All Mine	62
You Made me Brave	64
Who Wouldn't Want to be Welsh?	65
The Dawn	68
What Do You See When You Do Not See?	70

The Old Hat	73
I'm Not Old	74
By the Light of the Silvery Moon	77
I Will See You in My Dreams	80
I'm Doubting You	83
Autumn's Tree	85
But You Need to Know This	86
A Name Upon a Wall	88
If I Were a Pigeon	90
I'm Leaving You Tomorrow	92
It's Not as Easy as ABC	94
It is Not a Love Story	97
Kindness	99
Masquerade - the Great Escape	103
Forget Me Not	105
Misunderstood	108
Leaves	110
Modern Medusa	111
Just a Hand in the Darkness	113
I Would Rather Drop	115
That is a Question	117
Sleepwalking	119
Never the Twain Shall Meet	121
One Lifetime	123
The Glass Door	125
The Power and Price	127
Old Age is Not for the Faint Hearted	128
Moments that are Blown on the Wind	131
The Dinner Party	133
Snow	135
This Egg	136
This is What it is	138
Mrs Brown's Bucket	141
One Day My Life Will Become Landfill	143
The Grand Opening	146

Have Hope	148
My Forever…	150
Cut the Power	152
Fade Away	154
My Clock	155
For The Love of…	157
Forever and Always	159
Wish List - be a Lover	161
A Walk on the Dark Side	164
To be Valent	167
The Weekly Shop	170
~~GOLDEN~~	172
The Masterpiece	175
Creaking Doors	177
I had Waited for this Moment for so Long	179
Autumn	182
Hiding Tenaciously from the World	184
Every Picture	186
The Very Essence of Who I Used to Be	187
It's Your Loss	189
Song for Blake	192

In heartfelt dedication to Frances Margaret Jones.
Truly the most courageous woman I have ever met.
I could never have asked for a more perfect mother and role model.
For all the times I may have taken your love and your kindness for granted.
Thank you for sharing both halves of your life with me.
I will love you forever and always.
You made me brave.
I hope we make you and dad proud.

Butterflies and Feathers

I have a pot full of feathers
And a heart full of love
A red admiral butterfly
Sent from above
A head full of memories
In my dreams each night
You by my side forever
Rest now Mam, God bless, night, night.

We Did

I wanted to catch the sunlight
And watch as it danced and skipped lightly through your hair
Glistening and gliding through loosened curls of gold
Like fireflies on a journey to nowhere, already there.

I wanted to breathe your breath as sweet as the purest rose
As heady as jasmine and freesias caught on a summers breeze
Or a freshly cut meadow, as we gently fall to our knees.

I wanted to lie on tufted grass, wet with dew, with you
And melt into an abyss of the purest bliss
As we were blanketed in velvet, by the evening's dre
Just you and me.

I wanted to float with you, and soar with you
Amongst skies of golds and reds
On soft wide clouds to rest our heads
As the world unveiled its theatre
For us, its guests

I wanted to catch the stars and hand them to you one by one
To bask in moonlight as if it were the sun
To hide and seek with you in the darkened hues of a red blood moon
And to pause time, so it could never end too soon.

I wanted to kick the leaves of autumn with you
And place them gently back on the branches too
To freeze the frame and hold those autumn days at bay
I wanted to rewind autumn back to May
And to meet again in June.

And when the snow began to softly fall
In delicate flakes of the purest white
I wanted us both to see every flake
In a duvet day of snow , all cwtched up tight
And wonder in awe at how bright the night
When all we saw was light.

I wanted to... and we did.

As Goblets Fall to the Ground

Hell was lashing all around
Rain like goblets fell like shattered glass
To the ground
Crashing and thundering as it found
Its Armageddon!

As lightning flickered and flared
Its yellow eyes
Rolling across the skies
Illuminating the landscape
In freeze frames of time
Its breath as potent as a viper's bite
Billowed and blew black clouds of angry spite
Dissipating like burnt candy floss, tossed into
boiling, flaring seas
Bringing the whole world to its very knees
As it raged, its torrents of endless venom
Biliously puking its putrid contents to contaminate
all within its path
Contagious... using advantageous vantage points
To spew its contents, and spill its wrath

Until belly up, it lies like a ship beached
Beseeched
Urgently flailing in the light of day
As light, ethereal as angel's hair
Falls in strands and fills the breathless air
With hope and life
Whilst simmering seas, retreat and retract,
With steam as white as cotton wool
Dispersing in the full

Warmth of the day
Carried away
As if it were all just a dream

And the water, now filled with a million diamonds
Twinkles and glints with its endless chest
Of bounty, earned on this valiant quest
To banish this demon's soul
To renew and become whole
So when goblets once again
Fall to the ground
They shall not make a sound
As they melt, like sugar cane
In antidotal restrain
Surrendered! Surpassed and Supine!

Effortless

I woke up this morning
New silk dressing gown?
The only new one that I own?
Nope, I'm going for my old faithful wrap
It feels like heaven but looks like crap!

Breakfast over a chai latte today?
In a bone China mug of the most delicate grey?
Nope, a good old Glengette cup of tea
In a builder's mug we could swim in
You and me.

Then I comb my hair in the same old style
Put on my boots, weathered over time
Grab my handbag withered with wear
The leatherette missing here and there
Grab my coat and out I go
I've heard there's the faintest chance of snow

No effort or prep and there you are
Getting out of your battered old car
We hug and we kiss, and I laugh in your face
About your jumper and you say, "Get off my case!"
And then you take the mickey out of my creaky old knees
And we hobble to the café, and as you laugh you wheeze
And I laugh so much that a little bit of pee
Escapes, and again you're laughing at me!

We sit by the window,
Same old seats
That every Friday we sit in when we meet
The waitress comes over, "Same as usual please"
"No problem," she says "Thelma and Louise"
But we're more like Laurel and Hardy to be fair
Goofy and eccentric
But we don't care!

And we don't stop talking as time quickly passes by
And before we know it, it's time to say goodbye
And we argue and lament over who pays the bill
Each trying to pay as we fight by the till
And today I win, as I'm quick on the draw
With my credit card, and of course we then laugh some more

We walk to the car
And we hug and embrace
I wipe the cake crumbs from the crease in your face
You find my keys in the lining of my bag
And you mumble, I'm becoming "a decrepit old hag"
And then you disappear as you drive round the bend
How effortless to spend time with my dearest old friend!

Vampires Beware

There are vampires out there
Beware!
Hungry for their sustenance
Careless of their countenance
Ever ready to denounce.

Ravenously scouring their terrain
Those who remain?
In terror...sucked dry
Caught in the high
Of a feeding frenzy
That will neither satisfy, nor gratify,

Simply suspended
Until those incisors
Razor sharp
Sink into the very scarp
Of the jugular's soul
Devouring whole
Victims, unaware,
Until merely a shell
As soft as butter
Slowly drip... drip... drips...and melts away
In disarray
The slick...upon which
A naked flame, will engulf and swallow
Into the burning depths of hell
Those who fell

Hunting season is now
Unceasingly cruel, unforgivingly unkind
Maligned
So be alert!
Eyes open
Stand in the light warriors
Blaze bright
You are strong, fearless... perceivable
Primed to unyieldingly fight
Repel and retreat
The feat?
To liberate and extract those innocent souls
And crush those sharp incisors to dust
Restore the trust
Quell the hunger for mankind
Breathe the essence
"For the love of all, be kind"
And vampires?
Beware!
Warriors are out there
And hunting season... is now.

When the Windmills Cease to Turn

When the windmills cease to turn
I will be there
In the peace of the stillness
In the stillness of the night
Any night of a thousand nights
I will be there.

Where once there were
Cogs whirring
Hearts yearning
And sails turning
In perfect harmony
Like they would never cease to exist
And the winds would forever persist
To blow
For a lifetime.

Yet like electricity
Skipping in transmission
On a seemingly endless mission
Those countless gales
That blew for countless years
And countless sails
That soared through countless ears
of corn
Golden and in their prime
But feckless against time

Simply vanished, and ceased to be
The cessation of rotation
The death of a nation...
Of windmills that had danced in the breeze

And now...
The harvests have been reaped
And the sails hang in tatters on the mill
Ragged!
Abandoned!
A bitter pill
For a time that sailed through our destiny
But became a testimony
That all things must end

So...when the air is still
Listen!
Silently surrender
Hear the wistful whispers`
I hang, weightless in the air
For in the peace of the stillness
When the windmills cease to turn
I will be there.

What Happened to You?

Happiness is infectious
But hatred is contagious
A scourge in the propriety of man
I am not a fan.

The energy it sucks from the very soul
Leaves the shell wizened and worn
The contract of life torn
in two
Is that what happened to you?

A life wasted
On hatred
And inflicting scorn
When will it dawn… on you
That there is a better way?
Start today
Before it's too late
You choose your fate

The Very Next Station

She got on the train
Who was she?
Smartly attired
Possibly retired
An air of poise and grace
About her face
With a mere whimper
Of trepidation
And hesitation

She smiled, as the man
Took a stand
And proffered his seat
Where she duly sat to rest her feet
Took off her hat and settled down
Looked at the note in her hand
And with a frown
Noted the station
Of her destination
Leamington spa
So, not too far

They got chatting
And before too long
He had bid her goodbye
And he was gone
And now sat on the train
The colour drained...from her face

The truth of the matter
Was that whilst happy to natter
She had lost concentration
Invested in conversation
And now, everything seemed grey
Like she was a lifetime away
From where she was
Where she was going
Or where she had even been
Inwardly she screamed

She again looked at the note in her hand
Willing herself to understand
Under "Leamington Spa", It read;
"My name is Joan and I'm on an adventure.
It's hard for me, as I have dementia.
If I miss my stop at Leamington spa,
Get off at the next stop and don't wander far.
Ask someone to call this number below.
All I need to know...
Is I am loved."

She got off the train at the very next station
Then with poise and grace, and without procrastination
Handed over her note, and smiled, "I'm Joan
Will you help me please. I need to get home.
Because, I am loved!"

You Can't Argue with a Barcode

You can't argue with a barcode
Off to the reduced aisle with you
Past your best, and past your prime
Almost overdue
A pungent smelly piece of cod
Or a slimy piece of Brie
A squashed and damaged ready meal
Only good for today's tea

All popped in the trolley now
"Oh God!"
I think...
"That's me."

I just can't find my barcode
But I am definitely past my best
I can't see my best before date
Wouldn't pass a fresh squeeze test
But the thing about a best before
Is we all forget the after
The times we're in the "past it" bin
Are still filled with love and laughter
And I couldn't care less
If the manageress
Sticks a big sale sticker on me
I've got time to wait
Until my use by date
You can't reduce me
I'm free.

The Sun that Would Never End
Dreaming **E**very **M**oment, **E**ach **N**ight, **T**ogether **i**n **A**rms

And she was young today
Skipping through the tree lined hills
Giggling as she played, whiling away the day
In the sun that would never end

Glorious rays of golden light, shining bright
Until night
And it is cold
With aching bones
And rumpled skin, that creases and tears
Withered with wear
"Is anyone there?"

Where are you?
In an empty home?
Alone?
Crying and searching everywhere
He is not there!
Awake!
He is gone!
A month ago?
A year?
Yesterday?
Fear!

Dark, dark, night
And sheer fright
Hot sweet tea
Go to sleep, deep.

And the bells ring...

Oh, what a beautiful bride!
Filled with hopes and dreams
Eyes bright, open wide
Open heart, with love inside

He is there!
And together, stepping into the unknown
Fully grown
The whole world to own
Radiant and young
As one!

Ding dong, ding-ding, beep-beep-beep,
So long...alarmed!
It is morning!
Happy days... were yesterday
How grey the day, and skin, and hair
But he is not there!

Where are you?
And stepping outside through the snowdrops,
and the roses that he grew with such care
All those flowers... still there
Some for every season
To say "Hello... I'm here!"
Although he is not

The man that time itself, for her, forgot
But she did not!

He is alive!
Deep dive
Such a long, long day
And she slept awake with him
Walking amongst the scent and dew
When one became two

But that crying?
There, there,
Time for a bottle
And then we will play
All four together
As we dream the day away

So fast those days filled with laughter and fun
She's such a lucky one
Until one... in the morning
And then one is no fun

"Hello? Are you there?"
Careful on the stairs
Don't fall
Although Autumn is here
And Winter will claim the days all too soon
And it was,
All too soon,
As if it had never happened
And sometimes it didn't

But all too often it did
As day and night blur into one
There is more rain now than sun
Falling like tears to her breast
Bereft!

But why is she crying?
She doesn't know
Time to go,
Out with him!

"Are you ready?"
He is not there!
She wonders if she is there?
Sometimes she is
And sometimes a stranger invades her very soul!

But those beautiful hazy days
That flood over her like the sun
When she is young
They are there,
Always there
Like the garden in bloom
Always room... for her and him
The light is so dim
Until morning, night, night
Sleep tight
Tomorrow the forecast says sun
"Get ready" she says. "We'll have fun!"

Storm Alan

Snarling waves crashed,
Curling ferociously all around
Blocking any other sound
Barking and biting
Like a rabid dog
All teeth and foam
And the ship groaned
Aghast!
Their bloodshot eyes hovered on the abaft

They will never know
They whispered staccato, in the stilted hush
But the words were lost
Stolen by the bandit wind in its rush
To conceal those words
In the darkness of a tomb
And yet it would be dawn soon
Whilst a shaft of silky light
Permeated the night
Bringing sight
To those rendered dumb but not blind
Fearful to glance behind

"Aaaannnd cut!"
The director had spoken
And the storm had ceased
Anticipating peace
Only for another storm to begin
Steaming from within
Storm Alan
And he screams as he points the raft
To the now calm and tranquil pool
Upon which the abaft
Now rests
"Who the hell threw their Starbucks cup in the water?"
Bloodshot eyes and loose lips look and shout "Sir... it was your daughter"

Like a rabid dog
All teeth and foam
He stormed out... snarling ferociously home.

The Horizon

I took a picture
I touched the very edge of where the line held fast
That line, strong and bold
Although a little blurred
That entry to another world?

I can touch it; it looks like the end
Like you could almost trip off the edge into an abyss
Or bang your head on endless sky
A palette of greens, blues, and greys... drifting by
Without announcement or fuss, explanation or commotion
Not adrift in the ocean
But retaining all within and all without
To a world so far away... within reach.

I touch the line and run my finger across the ridge-less ridge
I push it a little... It does not budge
That seam of forever, standing powerful and strong
Stringing you along
Like a sentry, invisible unless you wish to pass
The line that, if you searched for, would move and quiver, like long green grass
So it would never be found, the groundless ground
A trick to the hapless eye, a visually virtual lie
And all as the waves gently lap at your feet
Lulling you gently to sleep
Until you relax.

Then the line is just a line
A horizon that we accept
A line in all but touch... except
We cannot find, or cannot touch
Only in this picture in my hand
The entry to another world, another land
The boundary keeper
Of a world so far away.

She Stood on Top of the Cliff and Waited

She had discovered the edge of the world
It was fraying a little
All jagged around the edges
With niches, and craggy ledges
Where one could sit atop, and stop,
And wait for a date
With destiny.

There is no halfway
All in, or all out
No place for error, misjudgement, or doubt
Just a faith to remain, to be caught, or to fly
A choice to live or die
And all as time ticks quickly by.

The water glistening below
Relayed a reflection
No time for deflection
Just that chance to begin right in the middle
To swim to the side
Or simply drown
Sinking solemnly down, down, down.

And as the dappled sunlight slowly meted, then melted away
Savagely blown to another distant world
The sky darkened and the rain began to fall
And as the rivulets ran ragged down her face
Everything she'd ever done, or felt, or even thought, she saw it all.

An awakening of sorts
She hoped she would be caught
But she could not remain
She could not be the same

Leaning into the wind
She had waited too long
She simply... let... go

And as the wind ceased to blow
And calm persisted all around
She fell, not to the ground
But into forever

Until the thermals caught her breath
In an almighty roar
And she soared.

Another dream
Another day
Perhaps another way?
Where the chance to remain...
Be caught, or fly
Was hers alone, her choice to live by.

The Fortune Teller's Crystal Ball

It was meant to be a bit of fun
All the fun of the fair
And as the workers called "Roll up roll up!"
She sat on her step with her long, matted hair
She didn't care!
After all,
She saw it all in her crystal ball.

They would come to see her throughout the day
Eager to hear what she had to say
The teller of fortunes come what may
The ball didn't lie!
But each time they said goodbye
She would smugly smile and sigh
"Why?
They come for my lies
Who wants to know that they are going to die?
Not I!"

They would sit engrossed as this woman would say
How her mother's, mother's, mother, had the gift
And it had passed through generations until this very day
But the gift were the lies from her cherry red lips

"The clue is in the detail"
Was what she would say
"They don't come to seal their own fate!
They simply want fortune
And that's what I sell
And that's why they queue around my old wooden gate"

So, as they sat and she steadfastly gripped her old ball
She eyed up what lies they should hear
The baby, the house and the nice little win
Would ensure their happiness for many a year.

But was it fortune or fate that sealed destiny?
Predetermined? Or do we make our own?
Was it a future these people wanted to see?
Or one they'd create when her seeds had been sown?
Who would really know?

Not her!
Nor did she care
The clock soon predicted
It's time they weren't there
And with a click and a chime
The mantle clock struck the hour
Just as she uttered "Come again my flower"

The ball, for a second, glowed a fierce amber red
And all of her fortunes suddenly flashed through her head
But as they left and she heard the clunk of the gate
She instantly knew, it was too little too late
Until now, she had never once seen her own fate
Had not even noted the date.

As the next clients stepped through that same wooden gate
Laughing and shouting "You go first mate"
The ball dropped to the floor, and she resignedly sighed
"I never predicted this," and she died.

The fortune teller was dead, and now they would say
How she had known she would die, but had still worked that day
And how her mother's, mother's, mother, had the gift
And now I have it too
Take a seat, and let's see what the ball shows for you!

The Hafod

The Hafod, where...
When the wind blows, you look like a film star
A natural facelift in the breeze
Looking ten years younger at least

Oh, how I hunger...

For that rugged wild landscape
Where eyes cry from the cold
But hearts sing at the view
Every season, fresh and new
Where grass is chartreuse, and bracken blazes like fire
Fences merely sticks, woven with wire
A visible barrier of no real strength
What animal would want to escape heaven itself?

The Lonely Shepherd standing erect and proud
Teetering above, like a misplaced phallus
Reaping views of the fertile land below...
unchallenged
Observing ramblers and hikers,
Cyclists and bikers,
Stop, to read the tiny wooden sign
Beckoning them to him
Should they relish the climb
And relinquish the time

Along the track-like roads
Walkers and dogs jauntily on their way
Could lose themselves all day
Yet not see a quarter, of what they ought to,
To do justice, and bank to memory, for a rainy day.

At the waterworks, eyes are drawn
To the opposing mountains terrain
As if a giant himself
Had once lived, conquered, and reigned
Angrily thumping his fist and imposing a dent... hell bent
Creating a crevice to last eternity, for all to see.

Sheep scattering like white dots
Across fields of crocheted meadow and moss
Perfect in its imperfection
Glowing in the reflection
Of the spring sun

Lower... and the wild suddenly dissipates and fades
The canal bidding a cheery hello on its way
As barges glide by, hosting mugs of tea
Dogs resting heads on knees
Meandering through life
No stress or strife
Watching everyone else rush on... missing it all

All the tiny little bridges, and windy roads
Secret paths, where lovers go
Hiding to make love beneath the stars
A perfect navy blanket concealing cars
With diamonds that light up the sky

This is God's country
The very best of his creation
Where man has made little input
To reap wrath or irritation
For here the hiraeth is strong
And only Nature belongs
In the very heart of the rugged, wild Hafod.

False Toothed Smiles

Lying in wait predatory
Creeping, and festering, beneath net and voile
Creaking and oiling, best before dated cogs
Concealed beneath age old masks, and false toothed smiles
And beneath layered time,
Rendering you walking stick weak, and geriatric meek.

Yet beneath the surface
The furnace flares and boils
Unchallenged, unseen to the naked eye
Or passerby
But not I
I am the life force
To reignite interest, redefine time.

Clink, clank bottle bank
Full today, out to play
Car key, key car
Flat tyre, won't go far
The law, ignore
Public order, harassment more
Layered lies, false prize, camera eyes
Lenses for all offences
False pretences

Arrested, protested, invested,
Finally bested
By self-owned, alcohol fuelled, tongue and lips
Mask slips
Rest awhile
For 18 months simply passed you by
Wasted!
In more than one way
Until the fire fades
To ember days
And simply burns away

If the Walls had Ears

If the walls had ears, would they have heard the builder
Proudly proclaim, that this best Beaufort brick
Deep red, dense and thick
Would build a fortress indeed
To fulfil all building needs
As he gently laid them down?

If the walls had ears, would they compare
All the families who had once lived there?
And secretly harbour a favourite and exclaim
"I liked them" ... but then complain
"I didn't like resident number two
So noisy they burnt my ears right through!"

If the walls had ears would they enjoy a good old fashioned row?
Taking sides on each side of the room
Of who would win this little vocal boom
Of noise and profanities
Only meant for certain ears
But certainly not for the wall
Who would of course judge them all

If the walls had ears, would it listen to all the love it held within?
Count every "I love you" and cherish the very moment they heard that love begin
Whilst listening to their music and wishing that for the love of God they had better taste
But realising musical maturity is an amble not a race

If the walls had ears what a privilege that would be
To be the voyeur that no one else would suspect or really see
But to have ears and no voice
Well how sad that would be?
Unable to heed, warn or join in
Having to accept whatever may be.

And if walls had ears how tragic at the end
When their own life is through, and the bulldozer ascends
How scary to hear your nemesis approach
And the crush of your soul when the wreckers encroach
And all that dense Beaufort brick of the most beautiful red
Has heard its last sound
And then the wall is dead

And all that history
The rows, the love, and celebratory cheers
Resting peacefully in the rubble
With the ears, that heard it all during all those years
But only in a world where the walls have ears

Folded, Crumpled, Creased, or Worn

Folded, crumpled, creased, or worn,
The encapsulation of hope in the amber light of dawn.
Or the glow from flickering flames in a barren land
Whilst in the depths of despair, in the palm of a hand.

Speaking a thousand words
Saying nothing at all
Sharing a thousand dreams
And holding them all... safe!

Held next to a heart,
To hear the gentle beat,
Willing it to live and to love,
In the face of defeat.

Always and forever by your side, on your side, and side by side
Bringing peace where there is nothing but pain,
Turning tears of fear and anger into salty rain
Rain that will bring rainbows of hope and joy where there is none,
And reminding you, you are loved, you are the one,

And that one faded, and battered piece of joy
That would mean nothing in a different hand, next to a different heart,
Is everything, the middle, the end, and the start,
It is the reason to survive, or even thrive,

And even on the darkest of nights
When it cannot be seen
It shines like a beacon of hope,
Through the restless dreams
Hand on heart, hand in hand, as one…safe!

And even when it fades and no one else can see,
You will! You will always see me,
In your hand, by your heart, or in your mind
It will always set you free.

Folded, crumpled, creased, or worn,
In the darkness of night, in the amber light of dawn
Forever… safe

I Once Gave You My Heart

I once gave you my heart
You placed it gently in your hand
Promising to love it, and be tender
I thought you would understand
It was yours to look after
For our "Happy Ever After"

But of course, you failed to see
The gentleness of my heart or me
And you closed your hand
Crushing both my heart and soul

And where once I was whole
You left me broken and incomplete
Unable to compete... with you.

I once gave you my head
I unburdened every thought to you
All my hopes, dreams, and fears
All my visions passing through
They were yours to share with me
Not to close your eyes so you could not see

I gave you all those thoughts that had once been only mine
Believing you would honour them, and think them divine
Not that you would share them like some Facebook post

And laugh at them, or jibe, or gloat
And so you abused my mind
And now I find
I cannot forgive... you.

So now I give you my bowel
Where I place all my waste
I give you all the shit that you gave me
And I rub it endlessly in your face
I enhance your natural aroma
And give you eau de faeces
I give you what you deserve
You repulsive fetid species
And as I expel you from the anus of my soul
I realise that in fact, I am whole
I have flushed you away
Taken back all that I had given you that day
And now I finally see
That I am over... you

Invalid or Invalid?

Today I wasn't me
I wasn't free
And I couldn't be
Myself.

Today I was frozen
In time
Pretending I was fine
But I was lost
Inside myself.

My greedy eyes absorbing life
As it ran on ahead of me
Until I couldn't see
What was next
Or even what had passed me by
And I sigh! "Aaaahhhh!"

My ears alert me
And divert me for a while
Chattering, nattering,
A smattering of life
As it goes on, and on, and on,
Around me
Noise surrounds me, but in my silence!
I see
I am invalid!

Sleep takes me
To a world beyond this world

And I run wild
As a child
Who had just found their feet
I run forever
Over the boundaries and lines
Which I cannot see over
I pass over
And surrender
To the joy.

Happy sleep ends
And upends me
I am in a prison of my own doing
And my own being
But soon I will be free
As the drugs decree
My sentence has been spent
And heaven sent
I am released.

These invalid days were only fleeting
I arise from this enforced seating
And feel alive
But what of the rest?
I was merely a guest
Of these patient lifers

Invalid or invalid?
What do we see?
Set someone free
Be there and validate.

In the Blink of an Eye

In the blink of an eye
We are born
We die
And all that is in between
Are the memories we make
The chances we take
And a vacuum of nothingness, and everything.

In the blazing heat of the summer sun
Fresh faced, hearts race, and days run...
Forever
Through the vacuum of springs and Autumns spent
Through reflection and repent.

Until those icy claws
Of the purest white
Dressed as a bride
In lacy guise
Slowly takes hold
Becoming bigger and bold
Until its veil covers the World
And it fades
Blissfully unaware
Until there is the nothingness; born out of everything.

Always late, always tomorrow
Fast forward, on, and on, and on,
But there is no rewind
No second take
Just that moment
A flash
To see our mistakes
And then the nothingness, that steals our everything.

Tick tock, every second like a heartbeat
Sometimes strong, sometimes weak
But always trying to speak
"Take your time", it would say
"Look... Don't, blink your eye!
Choose to live life, love life, see life, be life
For when you are tired by and by
You will blink your eye
And see the nothingness, that eats our everything".

In the blink of an eye
We are born
We die
And all that's in between
Are the memories we make
The chances we take
And a vacuum of nothingness, and everything
All in the blink of an eye.

Strawberries

One finds oneself in a right old jam
A somewhat sticky situation one might say
And although one's dignity is preserved
One feels undoubtedly unnerved
Discombobulated in every single way.

It jars one to say
One blames oneself things went this way
One got all fabulous, and juicy, plump and red
Too much lying in the sun
And sitting on ones curvy bum
Languishing seductively in one's lovely warm straw bed

One was used to being admired
Even squeezed and touched, desired
They just couldn't keep those fingers to themselves
Some would salivate and drool
And talk of picking me?
So cruel!
Then it happened
Now one is broken and bereft.

I mean one shouldn't be too sad
For they picked Doris, Gwen and Glad
And together we are in this sticky mess
But to squish one's juicy form
And to squash ones seeds and all
It really is not pleasant one must confess.

And so, in this new glass home
One finds that greedy eyes still roam
As they pluck our little jar up from the shelf
But in a quest to cause us strife
They really do stick in the knife
It's a situation one cannot condone oneself.

Today out came the farmhouse bread
And now Gladys is all but dead
Only a little piece of her is left behind
It is only time and grace
That is keeping me in place
As one squeezes ones derrière where one can hide.

And then "Salvation Sweet Salvation"
Are the words one dares to breathe
As out comes pastry, "Be still my beating heart"
One clambers to the top
And she spoons out a massive glop
It was ones lifelong dream to be a strawberry tart
One departs.

My Love, My Hero

Flowers planted gently in their beds
Tucked away, still warm from that bright summer's day
And they laughed and embraced as they patted the soil
And she smiled, and she blushed as she turned to say
My love, my hero!

That long hot summer
Lazy hazy days to roam
Tending their land, building their home
And the birds above sang as they swooped and they soared
And the sky lit up bright as thunder rumbled and roared
Across mountains and valleys and cities and towns
And time passed and winter would harden the ground
Creeping so softly, no warning no sound…

And it hardened the heart too
…All too soon.

Now those iron birds would regale the skies
Swooping and soaring in disguise
With engines, and sirens, and hatred, and guns
Deafening the screams of daughters and sons
Of those down below
Far away from their beds
Tucked away below ground
Darkness filling their heads
And she looked in his eyes
Patted her belly and smiled
My love my hero!

She left, and they cried as she carried aloft
Their garden, their home, in a brown plastic pot
New life, new hope, a new day to come
And he stayed and he wept at what he would become
Those long, grey days
With weapon in hand
Defending the home… their homeland
And her letter, and photo, of their much longed for child
Tortured his soul
And killed him inside
For he traced her words every day in the light
Heard them whispered in dreams long into the night
My love my hero…
But he felt it no more
For the villain inside was needed much more
This was war!

Then one day, the sun shone
And flowers swayed in their beds
He patted the soil as he laid down his head
Hot wet tears that would water the ground
A river of red, that ran silent... no sound
Except the distant words
My love my hero!

One day the birds did sing again
The sun shone so brightly, it hurt
She gently placed the pot on the ground
And patted the soil and the warm soft dirt
New life, a new start, in a land that was theirs
She watered the plant with her river of tears
She sprinkled his ashes in the beds that they grew
Knowing that new life from him would come through
She turned to her child
And blushed as she smiled
Reminding him again, as she had all this time
Of our love, our hero!

That long hot summer
Of lazy hazy days
In the land that was saved
Through the lives that they gave
And as birds swooped and soared
In the skies up above
There flew a solitary, pure white, dove
And it hovered, and waited, and exhaled all its love
Whispering my heroes my loves.

When Worlds Collide

East met West
But they knew best
Their journey, a quest
To unite not divide
As families, and cultures, and worlds collide.

>Radio blaring
>Sunlight glaring
>Two lives sharing
>Two worlds pairing
>On the road
>On their way
>That day!
>Tearing metal
>Searing heat
>Eyes meet
>Empty seat.

>Rushing on and on
>So much blood
>A flood
>And the light
>It's calling
>Heaven sent
>But the earth is crawling
>To circumvent
>What would become
>A battle as heaven and earth collide
>Will he decide
>The light or fight?

Stay another day?
Which way?

Rushing, rushing,
Beep, beep,, beep
Footsteps, screaming, faint heart beat
Please take a seat
She weeps
And steeped
In scarlet red
She holds her head
He's dead!
Except the faint heart beat
And incessant beep
As machines strive
To keep alive
What was declared and said
To be dead

In another world
Across the hall
They make a call

And in a darkened room
Of desperate gloom
The tomb
That has held a thousand days
And a hundred ways
To prolong a life
Is relieved of strife
The call cuts the silence like a knife
It's a match
And they despatch

Into the night
Towards the light
Where they will fight

Rushing, rushing,
Beep, beep, beep
We'll take it from here, please take a seat
And she weeps
As he's wheeled away
The chance to see another day
Their journey underway
She prays.

And somewhere in the abyss
Where heaven and earth
Hang on the precipice
Of two worlds colliding
Were two lives deciding
Their journey
Their path
And as they traversed
From dark to light and light to dark
They shared a moment
They shared their heart
But apart they continued along their way
Only one will see another day

Two lives sharing
Two lives pairing
Forever!

It's all over
And yet had only begun

Where once were two, now was one
And as they comforted and confided
Two women decided
Their worlds had collided
And forever, no matter how far apart
They shared a moment
They share his heart

In another world
On another day
On a different journey
Or a different way
Who is to say,
Who would stay?
When worlds collide

Those Eyes, Those Lies

The cloak is mightier than the dagger dares to be
Concealing in the shadows all those things the eyes can't see
A slight of hand
Or a hand well played
Out of sight, but not of mind
But the cloak will render those powerless
Those whom it chooses to render blind

Deceit and corruptness are merely the start
And the cloak conceals this well
But the eyes are the windows to the soul
And the eyes are where those lies will tell
So shake your cloak and wear it well
And keep those eyes shut tight
For the cloak is the bringer of darkness
But the eyes will be true in the light

You can blink, you can wink
You can even stare,
You can choose to look away
You can blaze those eyes of passion
Or you can use those eyes in whichever way
So you can convey
What you wish to say.

But remember those eyes are like windows
And unguarded, they open up wide
Other eyes will pry and stare right through the lens
Other eyes will see what the cloak failed to hide

So remember you sinners, and those with no faith
That the truth will outwit the lie
Beware of karma and the strength of the weak
And for those who will spy with their own little eye
For the cloak will be rendered powerless
A garment of duplicitous lies
For the truth will always rise to the top
And the truth will ooze from those unguarded eyes

You can blink, you can wink
You can even stare,
Or you can choose to look away
But the truth is held in the eyes to your soul
And they will display
What your lips fail to say

For the cloak may be mightier than the dagger dares to be
But lying eyes blaze like fires from hell
Until the truth will out, and only then will you see
That the eyes reveal truth, and deceive you as well.

There's a cold snap coming
So hold that cloak tight
Those lies tucked up safe by your side
For when you open those eyes
You will see the light
When you open those eyes, there is nowhere to hide
And finally, the dagger, is plunged deep inside
No more lies!
The truth of course lies in those eyes

The Guilt is All Mine

Finally,
I am alone
It is just me
But soon it will be YOU... and me

I reach out to you in the darkness
And we find each other
I whisper to you that there is no other
As I breathe in your heady scent
Heaven sent
Just for me... my very own

I move my fingers quickly and hastily
As I disrobe you
I absorb your nakedness
And wonder at your darkness
You are strong
But you cannot resist me
Any more than I can resist you
And... I break you

And when I know you are mine
I slide my tongue all over you,
You, taste exquisite
And I shiver at my greed
I know, I must have you tonight
I'm in too deep
My heart alight!

You surrender to me
As you always do
My iron will persists
As I nibble you
Gently at first
Until urgently I take you all
And like a female spider
I dispose of you...
Spent.

I lie back and wonder at my selfishness
But still, I lick my lips at the memory
Of you and me
And I see
That it is inevitable!
This is not the end
My need for you will overpower me
I will call for you again
And you will come

I climb the stairs to bed
Where my family slumber unaware
And... I do care!
The guilt is all mine
But... oh you are so divine
Chocolate, that delicious friend of mine.

You Made Me Brave

Yes... I was flung to the ground
And tossed
To the belly of that burning hell
That ate me up
And I was lost
Burning alive
As flames licked and laughed
Mimicking my terror
Holding me forever...
lost

But now I am brave
Invincible!
My armour shiny and new
I am brave because of you
I jump with both feet
Close my eyes and squeal
I welcome the storm
For I will overcome
I laugh at the rain
For it will precede the sun

I take chances
And I dance
To whatever tune plays
Never afraid
To shine.

Who Wouldn't Want to be Welsh?

Who wouldn't want to be Welsh?
To have the hwyl running through your veins
The land of Song
Where we sing before we speak
And even sing as we speak
"Ta ra, ta ra, ta, ra",
In a chorus of goodbyes
That you could only hear in Wales

Who wouldn't want to be Welsh?
The land of stories and legends
Where even the flag proudly displays a dragon
A beast that stands strong and proud
A red vision of strength
That says don't mess with us
We're Welsh

Who wouldn't want to be Welsh?
With daffodils and leeks proudly on display
Where we set aside time to celebrate St David's Day
And we dress as Welsh ladies and miners
Rugby players and line up
To be judged, on who is the most Welsh.

Who wouldn't want to be Welsh?
Where old pit heads, steel miners, and drams
Stand on mountains or in gardens
As a testimony and a celebration to the past
To all those who plundered the land
For the black gold
That kept a nation fed and warm

Who wouldn't want to live in Wales?
Where the miners' institutes still stand
Long after the mines ceased to be
To facilitate and celebrate all the things
That Wales has done well, and promises to be
Where pensioners can still be entertained
And have a meal and drink for free.

And being Welsh still means being stubborn and standing proud
We would not let our Welsh language die
We would not be oppressed, and now it survives
With words of beauty like "Cariad" and "Pili Pala"
A testimony to our valour
To remain Welsh, whatever the cost

And to this day as a nation
We are still obtuse
Where if we cannot win the rugby
We don't care if we lose
As long as someone wins… except jokingly the English.

Whose language we most commonly speak as Wenglish,
Who knew?

But the best thing about being Welsh is being home
In a land where the mountains are there to roam,
Casting shadows on the valleys
And the green lush grass below
Where the houses snake in never ending rows
Cwtched up tight, baking bara brith, and bake stones
To tempt us through our stomachs and our hearts
To be born Welsh what a privileged start!

Who wouldn't want to be Welsh?

The Dawn

The Dawn began, timid at first
A tiny light of amber rose
Gaining momentum as it grows
Glowing like a firefly
Straddling the horizon between land and sky
Dignified in its repose
Strands of light like magic flows
Kissing and caressing as it goes
Touching all, as it passes by
Rich, glorious and majestic throughout the sky
A fanfare of colour
A cacophony of light
The Dawn is here to end the cold night

Mature now, it blazes bright
Oranges, and golds, as Dawn takes flight
A Phoenix rising from the ashes of night
Regal as it smothers the darkness with light
Fingers of warmth to envelop the cold
Wiping the tears of dew as its heat unfolds
Awakening flowers as they unfurl from their sleep
Nodding their heads towards comfort and heat
The world has awakened, as it drinks in the Dawn
A new day, a new start, the light is reborn
And as Dawn is complete and the day is begun
We are ever grateful to Dawn for bringing the sun

The days are long and ever bright
Basking in eternal light
But as dusk falls
And darkness ensues
And hushes the world
With its gloomy grey hues
The world goes to sleep and closes its eyes
Awaiting the Dawn that will once again rise.

The Dawn is a Tigress to conquer its prey
The Dawn is a Phoenix to rise from the flame
The Dawn is a flame that flickers and glows
The Dawn is a fire gaining strength as it grows

And slowly through the chill of that long cold night
Through the black and the darkness, we can see the light
The Dawn is here to be glorious and bright
Always the Dawn to end the cold night.

What Do You See When You Do Not See?

What do you see when you do not see?
A gaze, a glimpse, a look, a backward glance
Those eyes that weep, and dance the soulless dance
A window, internal, and eternal, in the mind
Of passing moments, of all that's passed behind
A forward glance, to end the night-less dream
Where laughter ends and sorrow lends to screams
The lips that sowed the seeds that others grew
The eyes that saw the weeds those seeds would sow.

Fields of sorrow, as far as can be seen
Masquerading as the harvest of only dreams
Crops to yield, and feed the gluttonous few
Borne from the sweat and blood of those who never knew
A fertile soil of lies, deceit, and pain
Watered by the tears of human rain
A crop that will never fulfil and sustain
The hunger of the ones who live to reign
And to reign over, and make the rain of summers spent, and autumns yet to end
The storms that only nightmares can the terror lend.

And those who speak... shout
Whilst those who follow... lead
And those who see... eat
Whilst those who hunger... bleed

And those who have no choice, really do
And it is those, who chose not to choose, who...
See, when they do not see, fresh eyes with clarity
The zombies who rampaged through the dreams
And blew those nightmares apart at the seams.

And in the ashes, of what has been, and what once was
The tears turn to mud and slowly run away
Running from the eyes of those who see when they do not see
And yet whose lips will never say
A glimpse, a glance that eternal be
A hell to last for all eternity

And for those who were sleeping, and dreaming, and did not see
And those who worked the fields, and dared to dream the dream
May your dreams weather the rain that ran the rivers red
Let your eyes see only love inside your head
For what you see when you do not see
Are the choices you make

The actions you take
And all that has passed behind
Some will see forever joy
But others will go blind

What do you see when you do not see?
A backward glance of past eternity.

The Old Hat

"Take it! I don't care!"
Brooding anger flares
"It won't fit. You big headed Bastard"
Time to overshare
"Bastard you say? Really? Me?
The only Bastard here is the illegitimate you that I see
Ain't that right mam?"
Silence... then like a slaughtered lamb
Mam steps in
"Shut this bloody din
You two have no shame
Calling into question your daddy's good name
Yes there's been talk about your uncle Fred and me
But where is he?
Dead... Rapist pig
Dad made him dig
His grave... to save me
You see
Big head Fred
Is dead
Now he's just old hat
Fact!"

I'm Not Old

I'm not old
I'm like a peach
Firm with a hint of soft
With a little bit of peach fluff aloft
Here and there
But does it matter?
Who cares?

I'm not old
I'm like a ripened old banana
I've got a little sweeter with age
Not everyone's taste
My skin has even gone a little yellow
But I can still attract a fellow
And truly… who cares?

I'm not old
I'm like a fine wine
I've matured and gotten better with time
Fruity with a hint of life
With a twist of humour that can cut you like a knife
Would accompany a good Sunday roast
And make a good wife
Sharp, but not bitter
Mellow, and a real taste bud hitter
If anyone cares

I'm not old
Just everyone around me has got younger
And a little more stupid,
And thinner,
And quite frankly dimmer
Where's the life?
It's on the tablet, mobile phone and the like
Selfie? No thank you
I'm enjoying the moment
And so should you
But do you care?
Not yet

I'm not old
I'm just coming into bloom
Like a rose
I've opened up to life totally
And live life hopefully
That someone remembers to change the water
And care for me like they ought to
So I can grow old and droopy
With just a tiny hint of loopy
Let's hope someone cares

I'm not old
Just a little life worn
A bit cynical, sarcastic, sassy and satirical
A bit self-centred
Enough to wax lyrical
As for physical?
I'm a total wreck
First thing in the morning

Oh heck!
But after a bit of yoga
Life's a charm
What's the harm?
In self-care?

        I'm not old
        It's just an age
        It's just a number
        Another page
        In a huge long novel
        That I get to choose
        To be the heroine
        To win, not lose
        I'm not old
        Well not for me
        I'm just the right age
        That I am supposed to be
        And anyway
        I feel great today
        So am I old?
        Who cares?

By the Light of the Silvery Moon

The moon was full and bright
Beautiful, radiant, iridescent in light
And that night
Two hearts took flight
Gravitating together... alight!

It was lunacy they knew
Perfect strangers like magnets flew
Together in the rosy hue
Of a red blood moon
Both hearts would swoon
Until soon
It would be love

The man in the moon
Of course would see
That some things are just meant to be
And as the tide would ebb and flow
And the waves would come and go
Nothing could stop what we all know
To be the path of true love

Then one night after many, many, moons
That would wax and wane
The night became, intense, insane
And together in the dark
The eclipse of two hearts
Together entwined
Perfectly aligned
While the very stars that twinkled in repose
As Aphrodite herself on the back of Venus rose
To acknowledge what only lovers know
To be love

        That night the moon shone blue
          And together they knew
          They were no longer two
     And the love simply grew and grew
          Creating a moonbow too
          As the stars cried with joy
      A perfect girl and a perfect boy
           Luna and Selene
              A dream

For many years as seasons passed
The moon would light the way
But though the moon would never tire
The sun would seize the day
And then one night during the winter moon
As they stood by the old oak tree
They looked at the moon and both of them knew
That some things were meant to be
And as sure as time itself cannot be stopped
Nor love could ever die
Rebirth, new life is inevitable

As is the time to say goodbye

By the light of the silvery moon
As they hummed that same old tune
They watched as the stars shone one by one
And the full moons wolf howled too
Heads together, hands entwined
Their two hearts beat as one
And they acknowledged the moon gently slip away
To make way for the sun
And so by the light of the silvery moon
Their time on earth was done.

I Will See You in My Dreams

I will see you in my dreams
And I will walk with you
I will stare at your face
And I will remember you,

We will laugh
And I will remember the sound
Storing it in my mind
So it is forever around,

I will ask you all the things
I should have asked before
And tell you all the things
I should have said and more,

And I will listen like it's the last time
And I will give like it's the only time,

I will hold your hand
And remember your soft loving touch
And I will put my arm through yours
As we loved to do so much,

I will rest against your cardigan
And feel its warmth again
And I will breathe in deep
To hold on to your smell,

And when I hug you
I will remember it
It will feel like home
The way you hold me
Every muscle, every bone,

I will hold that hug forever
To last the end of time
I will hold you in my dreams
I will forever know you're mine,

And though you are not here
You are beside me
And when I close my eyes
You will be there
And when I need you
I know you will carry me
You would take me anywhere,

I will talk with you, and talk about you
And always hold you in my heart
And although this time you had to leave
We need not be apart

I will see you in my dreams
And I will walk with you
Hand in hand
Arm in arm
Holding you
And I will remember

You will always be there
My beautiful butterfly, you're everywhere

I'm Doubting You

Dancing provocatively
Arching, bending
Swirling seductively,
Salaciously ending
With a burning desire
Rising ever higher
Splattering charcoal shadows across the wall
Casting secret spells upon all
Who dare
To longingly stare
Sucked in for sure
By the tantalising hypnotic allure
Of ever changing beauty within

                Regally you soar
          Mocking those peasant moths
           Who frantically flutter by
             And wonder why
         They cannot avert their eyes
              It's no surprise
             Ancestors of old
            Were bold enough
            And cold enough
              To risk it all
                For you
           Then… have it all
             Because of you
           You powerful being!

Oh amber glory
Defiantly painting a story
Uninhibited, unrestricted, unrestrained
How you quiver
As you draw beads of sweat to my brow
As only you know how
You swell and retract
Teasing, Appeasing, Pleasing
Ever seizing... the moment

Your intensity overpowers
And devours the air surrounding you
I exhale sharply,
To
Drown
You

I know how you work
I've looked at you
Looked into you
And looked through you
Now I'm flaming done with you

I doubt you ever noticed me
Now, I'm doubting you
Play with fire, and you will get burned
We're over
And you're out.

Autumn's Tree

As Autumn ensues, the leaves are gilded golden brown
The soft tender leaves release and tumble to the ground
Becoming crisp as they lie bereft on cold, hardened floors
Crunchy beneath feet, not young or supple anymore
Branches become brittle, bare, exposed
As the jewels they held dear, simply offload
For some years, Autumn winds have passed us by
Leaves on my precious tree have held on tight
New leaves formed on branches way down low
New branches, making room for them to grow
Now Autumn winds blow, we endeavour to hold fast
To remain within the present, not the past
To survive the Winter, the hardest tree of all
The family tree that strives to survive the Fall

But You Need to Know This

I didn't know there were psychopaths walking amongst us
I didn't know how some people got their kicks
I didn't know boredom breeds contempt
I didn't know some people are born evil, and some are just sick.

I didn't know you could receive nourishment through others' destruction
Or that some amongst us, gain joy from others' pain
I didn't know that some plan the downfall of others
And I didn't know that some block the sun, just to bring the rain.

>But for all I did not know
>I now have gained
>For all those lessons learned
>I now am saved.

>You have shown me all these things
>That my eyes had failed to see
>I now see that knowledge is power
>And now that knowledge will save me.

I do know that Albert Einstein was right
Evil will not destroy the world alone
But watching evil and standing by
Would make the world a place that evil owned.

Yet certainly of all the things that I have learned from you
It's about time, that you also learned a lesson too
You need to know this, for your will I cannot allow
I will not just stand by, and I am coming for you now.

Psychopaths walk amongst us
Along with evil, sick kicks, and all
But now I make a stand
Now I make you fall
The truth will prevail after all.

A Name Upon a Wall

I don't want to be a name upon a wall
Nestled amongst my good friends after all
I don't want you to search my name and weep
Because of promises I made, but I could never keep
I don't want your fingers to trace my name engraved
Or you torment yourself... for I could not be saved
And I don't want a cold stone wall to ever be
The place you come to mourn and remember me.

I want the flowers that we share to be alive
Like the poppies in the field, past where we loved to drive
I want your visits to be everywhere we went
I want your memories to be filled with all our moments spent
I don't want stonewalled silence to be our new reality
I want us laughing, holding hands, eating ice creams by the sea
And I don't want strangers come to visit, stop and stare
I don't care, I am not there.

This is not the way my life was meant to be
But that's the price we paid for others to be free
And yet to fight, for peace, was always so perverse
Whilst the greed and pride of man remains a curse
So please don't see my name upon the wall
Nestled amongst my comrades who also had to fall
Please see my name in dreams of you and me
And remember to love someone like you, I fought to set you free.

I might just be a name upon a wall
But my head is high, chest out, and I walk tall
A cold stone wall is where my name might well forever be
But in your dreams I am alive… in happy dreams remember me
And for all the seeds of poppies ever sown
The message when they bloom is that I wish that I had known.

If I Were a Pigeon

If I were a pigeon
I would tour the world
With my navigational skills
I'd watch the universe unfurl.

I would soar amongst the pyramids
And flutter in the dunes
I would escape the wintry grey UK
And return for the summer solstice moon.

I would see Canada and America
Taking in all fifty states
I'd flap around the Champs-Elysees
And eat garlic, snails, and crepes.

I'd become the bird Prime Minister
And my parliament would say
That cats would have their claws removed
And I'd banish birds of prey.

I'd make it legally blinding
That humans would share their chips
So that all pigeons by the seaside
Could enjoy these fatty bits.

And if I were a pigeon I'd make sure
You were always by my side
My feathery little partner
With whom I'd mate for life.

We'd raise a little chick or two
And although we'd love to roam
We would always be together
It would always feel like home.

And after our six years were done
Which isn't very long
We would go to pigeon heaven
Where our love and lives live on

I'm Leaving You Tomorrow

How could I say those words to you?
And, if I had said them, what could you do?
What words could pass between us that exist
That could have stopped this?
Instead
We have all these words left unsaid
Countless notes of love unread
And you lie alone each night in bed
Silenced.

And the silence engulfs us like a wave...
Of all the words I gave... to you
Except those few.

"I'm leaving you tomorrow" would have hung in the air
And slowly, choked us both

We would have died a thousand times
Before tomorrow had begun
We would have cried a thousand nights
Until that first glimpse of sun
Arose over the mountains that we loved
Drying the salty dew
That covered me and you

And still...
What words could encapsulate a lifetime, or promise eternity?
What words could pass between you and me
That we couldn't already see?
You are all my words

    So yes, those words remained unspent
    Tomorrow came and went
    As did I
    I left you yesterday
    But I never went away
    I lie with you
    In the silence... always

It's Not as Easy as ABC

It's an affliction
Like an addiction
A coercive control of the mind
A beautiful mind
That is cowed to feel
That it must heel and heed
To the warning indeed
That only exists
In your beautiful mind

Constantly nagging
On and on
Until it conquers
Then all hope is gone
And another day has passed to night
Another day to face gaslight
Hold on tight you
Tomorrow is déjà vu

The secret that is hard to hide
From those who are close and see inside
But to others a facade is all they see
They don't see you
They don't see me
Fighting the fight
Sending you light
To beat the darkness, as black as the darkest of nights
Torturing your soul
Stealing your sleep
Cowing the lion, to a lamb or a sheep

But now you stand up
You have taken a Stand
The lion has been sleeping
Now it's surveying the land
It roars at the lamb
And the lamb runs away
It sneers at the sheep
For the sheep it will slay

Ferocious and hungry from a life that was starved
A life full of limits
A life that was halved
Three little letters but not ABC
For today the alphabet
Does not belong to thee

You conquer, you deafen the voice that has been
You close your eyes to all you have seen
You are deaf, you are blind, you have taken control
You have found your voice
You have reached your goal

Victorious you rise
Free, to be free
A life without limits
Your life you decree
The battle is over
The war has been won
You are the conqueror
You are the one

A hostile invader
That crept up over time
But was finally quashed
By your beautiful mind
Now you hear clearly
Now you can see
That this life is yours
Now you are free
The victor the hero
No more OCD

It is Not a Love Story

Life is precious
Transient and fleeting
Humanity united through hearts filled and hearts beating
To the purest rhythm of life in motion
Moving forward with the notion
That life is love
And in its truest glory
Life is a love story

    And yet, every day, in a different way
    We see that same utopia
    Ruined by the myopia, of mankind.

    How could we fail to see
    The atrocities throughout history?
    And still deny
    And still believe the lies
    Yet rarely question why.

    Then like a film on rewind
    Mankind
    Will still replay the narrative
    Inciting the inflammative
    And reliving time…
    Time and again.

I spy with my blind little eye
Nothing,
For those on high
Will turn their blind eye
Whilst innocents die.

We allow this quest for power
We permit the greed, and dismiss those it might devour.
It is this never ending search for ultimate glory
We close our eyes to all things predatory
And sadly that is not love, it's a travesty
And a self-written, unedited, murder story.

Kindness

I walked contentedly today
And a little bit of kindness came my way
From when I opened the door to go outside
And the postman passed and waved and smiled.

        I continued to walk along the lane
    And a little bit of kindness came my way
And as the chill of the air enveloped my skin
   Freezing my bones and my organs within
  The sun my good friend held out her hands
        And wrapped me up warm,
      As she caressed the land.
         Kind, kind, sun.

As I smiled and absorbed all the kindness around
A little white feather raised up from the ground
Dancing and twirling as it rose on its way
Tickling my nose and my brow and I say
To myself of course,
"Why thanks little feather"
For soaring and flying and floating wherever
And reminding us how much we love to be touched
On our skin, in our minds, in our hearts, oh so much.

Jauntily now I bob on my way
Lifted and buoyed by the joy of the day
And over the noise of the bustle and sounds
A sweet melody echoes all around
A song and its notes fill my ears and my soul
And I dance from within, feeling complete and whole.
I look up to see that chirpy little chap
Fly away with his partner and I cheer and I clap
To myself of course
But all the same
That little song of kindness had come my way
Bringing joy to my heart and love to my day
Sending me skipping along and away…

And into the café
For a quick morning treat
Ordering a milky hot chocolate and taking my seat
As the girl at the counter sleepily beavers away
Preparing my order, the first of the day
And brings it to my table with a cheery "Enjoy"
As she walks away singing, I look and I smile
In my mug is a heart sprinkled brown on the white
Love and kindness has been shown, just that extra little mile
And as I leave her a tip , I walk off with a smile.

On my way home, a bird's nest I see
And I whistle a song to the cute bird's baby
So it can see happiness and joy coming its way
Just a little bit of kindness to cheer his day.

On I walk and the air is now, oh so still
And at the very next window, there on a sill
A little white feather, grounded in place
And as I walk towards it at a leisurely pace
I purse my lips, and very gently I blow
And smile as the feather lifts up as it goes
Upwards and onwards, twirling at speed
As it floats on the thermals to someone in need
Of touches and tickles, so they too can say
A little bit of kindness came their way

And now for the sun
Thank you my friend
I'm warm to the touch and glowing as well
I open my arms
And give salutation
That long may you glow across every nation
I see you sun, and all the work that you do
And I've taken time to say "Thank you" to you
What a beautiful, wonderful day
And I can spread kindness in my own little way.

There's the postman, on his way home in his van,
Looking tired and weary as all of us can
So I stop and I wave and shout "Have a great day"
And soon he is chuckling, as he drives away
And I'm sure he mouthed, though I couldn't hear him say
How a little bit of kindness had come his way

Kindness is free, full of joy, full of love
Coming upwards, and sideways, and sent from above
But all of us have that kindness within
And as we spread it, and share it, all of us win
Tomorrow as you begin your day
Spread a little bit of kindness along the way
It will come back to you always, and you too can say
A little bit of kindness came your way.

Masquerade - the Great Escape

I am a criminal as I masquerade through life
Many faces, many places
I am prolific
My misdemeanours rife.

Ill qualified am I
Which I skilfully disguise
To ensure my demise
Through ineptness
Will never arise

Confidence exudes me,

I fill a crowded room
As I raucously laugh and boom,
With my loudness
Carelessly, caring less, what others think
Or how much I drink

I have all the answers
That others command of me
And demand of me
My opinion is, valid
And never pallid, as I strive
To fulfil expectation
For the duration

I work the long shift
Play the long game
Until tiredness descends
And upends me.

The heels are off
The red lipstick smeared away
Call the police
She's escaping and getting away
999
There's a crime
Yes, I'm calling it in.
I never planned it officer
Yes, I was coerced
Yes... That's right
No never at night
At night I really am me
What? A dichotomy?

I mean who even is she?
In the boardroom, in the bedroom
And no one gives her headroom
Yet she smiles
As she glides...
Away

Until the blue lights flash
She makes a dash
Stop imposter!
Someone, accost her
She's gotten away with it...
Again.

Forget Me Not

All day birdsong
Loud, fresh, and clear
Happy in the burning sun
Spring's promise that summer will arrive
Bursting with pride
Its beauty surpassed by nothing that time could reveal
Or secrets unseal

Forget-me-nots jostle for space
Each minute flower in its own place
Saying "forget me not"
For those whom time, may one day have forgot.

And as evening draws ever closer
And the sun burnishes from gold, to orange, to red
We remember, that as we live and wake, others go to bed.

The mountains scarred with tracks from those who live
Stands proud, healing its scars, time to forgive
And the skies... never so blue
Never so clear
Skilfully disguising
What is near
What we fear
What is here.

In this perfect world
In this perfect time

Nature has reclaimed its place
Taken back its space
Moving at its own pace

And only by the grace...
Of God himself
And those who care
And are there
Heroic in their plight
To stave off the long cold night
And lend a hand
And hold a hand
And embrace the night
So that we can reclaim the day
Reclaim the sun
And encompass the dawn
And the forget-me-nots
Who might otherwise forget you

And though we hide
Even from the ones we love the most
We choose to live as ghosts...
Than to be a ghost

So, for now, the shadows must keep us safe
And we hide away
Ever grateful to see the new day
So that one day
When we are full...
And have learned the lessons of this day
It might just go away
Then we can live
Side by side

With nature and with pride,
Love and be loved by those for whom we care
And those we choose, for our lives to share.

And so, life isn't fair
And many who are loved
Will not live to see the brand-new day
Chosen too soon...
Before the summer could begin
Before the world could heal
And before the sun could raise the heads
Of forget-me-nots, in their beds.

But we will not
Even when we're old and grey
Forget them, forget this day
Forget this time, when life stood still
Or even stopped... for some
But look...
There's a rainbow
And there is the sun.

Misunderstood

We must fight for peace
Shout to regain silence
Be firm to tame the beast
And be strong to quell violence.

We smile to hide our hurt
And cry when we feel joy
We hide when we are lonely
And we rebuild what we destroy.

We lie awake when we are tired
And eat when we feel fat
We cannot wait to share our secrets
And we can argue with a fact.

We speak when we have nothing to say
Remain silent when things should be said
We do not talk to our relatives when they are alive
But we visit the grave to talk when they are dead.

We waste time when we have none
But time drags when we are bored
We spend money that we have not got
But when we are rich, we hoard.

We holiday to get away,
But always carry our baggage
Then we let off a massive life bomb,
As we struggle to limit the damage

We say yes when we mean no
We say no when we mean yes
We sometimes laugh to hide concern
We clean up, but then make mess

We wait for sun but sit in shade
Remember what we would rather forget
We never take chances, but we ask for a chance
And we gamble if it's a safe bet

Then we complain that we are misunderstood
But are confused as to why this is the case
And the person you tell this to would agree with it all
Because they can tell you the truth, when they lie to your face.

Leaves

Leaves...
Crunching underfoot on a crisp Autumn Day
I just love it that way
Nothing gives me more pleasure
Than at my leisure
Kicking up my heels
With delighted squeals
As layers of nature's confetti
Float all around
And I dance a little bit inside
Trying to hide
The child
That's inside us all
As they swoop and fall.

Modern Medusa

Modern Medusa would have ringlets of gold
Billowing defiantly as she rode
Roughshod over every man, boy, or belligerent male
Who dared degrade women and then regale
Their innocence as if by default
The female is to blame
Simply because
She was captivating
Not titillating
And certainly not a vessel
To be used, abused and vilified
Denied the right to state, she was in fact defiled
And all in the name of pride
And of course, the birth right of man

If Perseus and Cellini were alive today
They would not with a severed head portray
The shame of women, taken by force
They would see of course
A beautiful woman with head held high
They would be held accountable, and be questioned "Why?"
And all the time she would hold their gaze
Her powerful stony expression alone would faze
The most resilient and heartless of men

Today Athena would be pictured hand in hand
With Medusa as together they took a stand
Against violence, abuse, and oppression

To make an impression
On every female to be strong
          For they are not wrong
     And Poseidon would be revealed as a snake
                 amongst many
           Whilst Perseus her enemy
        Would hold his own head in shame
             Realising the game
    Was finally up for arrogant, ignorant men

Today Medusa would be supported
Poseidon's crime reported
And although it might not make prosecution
It would be one step further towards legal and moral persecution
Of those who act because they can
And for that reason, every woman, child, and man
Would review the evidence and say, on this day
Medusa, hold your head high
Let your hair fly
You are a heroine

Just a Hand in the Darkness

Just a hand in the darkness
Connecting
Just a whisper in the air
Protecting.

Rustle of sheets
Heaviness of breath
Entwining of feet
And then the breadth
Of memories and emotions
Washing in like the tide
Tumbling from inside
All the times we laughed
And those times we cried
All those days true
Spent forever with you.

And now you gently brush the grey away
And caress the skin that seems to fade each day
You bring the roses to my blush
And in the hush
And the stillness, that has followed the day
You hold our tomorrows at bay.

And then when the Dawn finds us both asleep
Gently in our slumber
I awake and wonder
How you touch the darkness and make it bright
And I know we're alright.

It might not be as steamy now for you and me
But you see,
I know every wrinkle and every line
I remember every moment and every time
That you made my heart skip a beat
And race in the heat
Of a long summers night.

> And so tonight
> I will hold on tight
> As I always do... to you
> And reach in the darkness
> For your hand.

I Would Rather Drop

It was perilous
Hanging head first off that cliff
But still querulous
My other half went headlong into it.

If only I'd worn different boots
Or walked without a gait
If only we'd set out earlier
Why was I always late?

If only I'd walked slower
I was always in a rush
If only I'd planned out the route
On and on she fussed.

If only it was warmer
Then she wouldn't be so cold
If only we were younger
Really, we were too old.

If only we had a signal
Or our mobile phones were better
If only she'd married someone else
Who wasn't such a fretter.

If only we'd joined a knitting group
Left the walking to the walkers
If only we'd gone out with our friends
She had always been a talker.

And on, and on, and on, she went
I couldn't take it any more
Now she was gonna have it
Before I dropped and hit the floor.

"Right you whinging whining woman"
I bellowed very loud
"If only you'd bloody help me"
Well her jaw just hit the ground.

We weren't a million miles away
We had hardly walked Ben Nevis
And really it wasn't much of a cliff
More like a little crevice.

But before I continued the rant of my life
A voice came from below
"You alright there mate? Do you need a hand?"
And with that I just let go

I'd rather drop than face the wife
With her anger as black as night
If only I'd kept my mouth shut
And kept my lips shut tight.

And now she's looking down on me
As she has done all her life
If only I had married someone else
Instead of my quarrelsome, querulous wife.

That is a Question

To heat or not to heat?
That is a question
Or to eat or to not eat?
That is a question too
But not a question we expected to ask in 2022
And then as we rumbled on through 2023
A question we must ask ourselves
Is...When will the end of all this madness be?

In a world where we wage war, to have more
And greed is a quest
Where dictators dictate
Because they always know best
Where the poor are oppressed
Whilst the rich become mighty
Where influencers influence
And politicians are flighty
Where the land spews volcanoes
And the earth quakes at night
And famines and floods
Are a regular sight
And huge fires rage to blacken our land
Whilst fish choke on plastic as they die on the sand
And rapists keep raping, and paedophiles exist
And knife crime and neglect befall innocent kids

And whilst poverty and deprivation reverberate around
There are plenty who have never valued the pound
There is the divide between the rich and the poor
Where the poor seek existence, and the rich just seek more
And whilst in St Tropez, steering the yacht
The world is a playground where the poor are forgot

So to eat, or to heat, or to merely exist?
Is not a question but a struggle that continues to persist
For although we're all equal when we are born and when we die
When we live, life is not fair
And the question is…Why?

Sleepwalking

Sleepwalking as if it were forever
As if change had ended
Superseded by status quo
And all the while
It was just a dam
Holding…

Holding onto the picture
And freezing it in time
Before letting go
And in the flow
It is time to swim
Or drown in the effluence
Of our own doing
A septic tank
So rank
The space to breathe is lost

Time had moved on
Shifted… and stolen the place
Carefully bookmarked by us
For us
Gone forever.

>And like all perfect things
>It must all end
>Until we find our new beginnings
>And rebuild again.

A place where we can sleepwalk as if forever
Behind our dam
That will hold it all
Just for a while
So we can breathe
Hold onto the picture
And freeze it in time
Holding...

Never the Twain Shall Meet

The sun arose
Bursting into glorious light
Straddling earth with its amber delight
Setting the world on fire
Ablaze
Burning the black velvet curtains of night
Leaving a smoky haze
To settle on all below
Aglow
Awakening from slumber.

Victorious, it shuns the moon
Who often attempts to rise too soon
Especially on cold winter nights
When the sun is too weak to fight
Allowing the black velvet drapes to fall once again
Without restrain
Illuminated
By the blue, white hue
Of a full round moon.

And so it was that never the twain shall meet
And each dawn and dusk
The sun and moon
Would hover on the cusp
Of a new day, and a new night
Never losing sight
Of their opposing views
Or how they saw the world
In a different light.

But secretly the sun
Admired the calm of the moon
And would often swoon
Wishing for a glimpse of the night
Whilst the moon
All quiet and mellow
Would secretly long for the joyful yellow
That the sun would bring.

Until one night, or was it day?
The sun seemed to get in the moon's way
And as they awkwardly danced about
All the lights when out
And the whole world held its breath
And in that moment… that neither sun nor moon would ever wish to miss
They came together in a cosmic kiss
That set the universe alight in its delight
And this they deemed the eclipse.

One Lifetime

I can't remember much of her before
Perhaps I would have tried if I had known what lay in store
But I can't remember much of her for sure
Yet I know that she is not here anymore.

I knew she had disappeared straight away
I recall saying it out loud on that specific day
But loss is an emotion we choose to just ignore
I accepted it… I didn't know her anymore.

Pictures, flashbacks, stories, left to share
They help remember once that you were there
The way you'd sing, or cook, or laugh, or drive, or dress
But the person, I remember less and less.

Yet the one thing that you hid, that I couldn't see
Was the fact that you had also forgotten me
Yet you made out, you had remembered all that time
And I pretended you were still there, you were mine.

And in that moment, a lifetime was set aside
And everyone around you, joined the ride
And for a long while, emptiness ensued
But slowly, you remembered... and then we saw the brand new you.

Different memories, different stories, but a lifetime left to live
To share a lifetime is a gift, and it's all we have, to give
To get to know each other, love each other, and now it's so clear, its true
One lifetime, two mothers, and both of those, were you.

The Glass Door

So, I regarded the street full of coloured doors
Green, red, blue, white, and a glass one from top to floor
And I wondered what all these colours had to hide
And if the colour matched the mood of what it held inside.

The green one? Was it calm and peaceful too?
Or full of jealousy, and envy through and through?
Or the red? Was it an angry living hell?
Or warm and vibrant, full of chilli pepper smells?
The blue one might be cold and heartless, full of ice
Or filled with blue skies, oceans, beaches, and all things nice
And the white one? Was it clinical, sparse, and clean?
Or sparkling full of freshness, the likes of which you have never seen?

But what about that lovely clean glass door?
Surely an open book is what would lie in store?
A glass door would have nothing left to hide
A glass door would have lovely things inside
But when the lights go out, the glass is black and dre
Then through its glass, no-one else can see
No-one knows the things that lie in store
Behind a black and darkened top to toe glass door.

Appearances are deceptive, and in the light
We only see what others wish to put in sight
So beware of people solely made of glass
And give them a wider birth, when you need to pass
They may not be as transparent as they seem
Or as clear as the shiny glass would deem
The glass can darken, and shatter into shards
To puncture the joy that lives within your heart
The glass door is often never as it seems
The glass door can be the thief to steal your dreams.

The glass door, by day, the most beautiful and bright
But fear the glass door, and do not knock on it at night
The glass door, the most visible of all
The glass door, the impenetrable wall.

The Power and Price

For the times we made it
For those we love
For rebirths and new births
For those in heaven above
For all the chances taken
We never passed up
For when we were brave
And never gave up
For who we became
When we could have been lost
But also... for those we let go of
Without counting the cost
For all the "Sorry's", we should have said
For the times we turned our back
Hiding tears we wouldn't shed
Holding hearts afraid to crack
For all those ups and downs in life's crazy ride
Thats the power... and price... of pride

Old Age is Not for the Faint Hearted

Old age is certainly not for the faint hearted
Checking your pants
To see if you have followed through
Whilst hoping you have only farted.

Waking up in the morning
And pulling the curtains aside
For the mirror to reveal
There's been another land slide…

On your face
It's a disgrace!

And balance? Oh, don't get me started
What the hell happens to that overnight?
Where you shuffle sideways like a crab on steroids
Whilst trying to pull on your tights.

Then everyone's names, seems to blend into one
And you lose a hundred words everyday
And without your glasses you're virtually blind
And you can't hear a word that anyone says.

Your knuckles are gnarled
And your liver spots are plenty
Your bones creak and crack
And you are running on empty

Your patience is waning
And your feet are like leather
And one unkind word
Can knock you down like a feather.

The internet is a mystery
And Apps should be banned
And why not use words
Emojis should be canned.

And a really good day out
Apart from shopping for food
Is a bloody good funeral
To get you in the mood.

For writing your will
And then you reflect
That you've worked all your life
And all that is left.

Is your money, your house
And a few knick-knacks to boot
And yet your whole life
Was spent planning this route.

For when you could retire
And slowly grow old
Like a well preserved fungus
Or a fast growing mould.

But then when you get there
You just want to turn back the time
Erase every grey hair
Delete every wrinkle and line.

But there's no time to think
Because you have just drunk your tea
And you're crossing your legs
Because a trickle of pee.

Has just escaped that pelvic floor
That you had said you'd keep tight
So now you must hold the dam
With all of your might.

Because there's nothing worse
Than sitting on a mobility scooter
With a crotch full of pee
That is rotting your hooter.

So yes growing old
Needs a strong heart to be sure
And a reinforced gusset
And a strong sense of humour.

But at the end of the day
When all has been said
I would rather be old
Than the alternative, dead.

Moments that are Blown on the Wind

And there ends the chapter
Another family fractured by death
The final moments of a story
In a person's dying breath.

And as the home is all but emptied
And possessions dispersed
So too are the memories
Scattered into a myriad of bursts
Of moments that are blown on the wind.

As it was always meant to be
Fulfilling the prophecy
That despite those precious times of joy and love
We will all succumb to reside above...
This mortal earth, where all those we loved and knew
Perhaps still continue to live, just as they have to
As though those who departed
Were simply passing through.

And just by chance and luck alone
Were these people our heart and home
On loan
Like precious books
Removed from a library to read
Every page planting a seed
Of what would begin, what would become, and how it would end

But what a book
A heart wrenching page turner of love and loss
Hopes and fears
And holding near...
Those who we will ultimately lose
But always choose
To remember... In the moments that are blown on the wind.

The Dinner Party

Six chairs at the table
In two rows of three
Plus one at the head
To host, and oversee.
Seven glasses, seven napkins
And cutlery galore
Six candles in a candelabra
To be lit just before
Six place names written neatly
With letters of Gold
By the host in calligraphy
The writing of old
Peter Williams with Glenys
And Phillip Pearce with Fay
And finally, Alex Murphy
And his lovely wife May.
Dinner cooking
Pots steaming
Oven roaring to life
Timers dinging
Host singing
Meat carved with a knife
Music playing
Host saying
Dinner is now ready
One plate, and one dinner
Placed carefully and steady
Candles lit
Wine poured
In seven glasses but none
Of the six will be drinking

Only the one
To good friends past and present
Fondly announces the host
As she gestures to all of the chairs
In her toast
And to all those who are absent
May I just say
For the rest of my life
I will host you this day
For seven passengers , one car crash
One mangled old wreck
Thirty years ago, six passed
And one heart bereft
So for one day each year
Until forever is done
The dinner party set for seven
Will be eaten by just one

Snow

Snow
Why do you descend so nimble?
What is the hurry?
So beautiful in your flurry
As you whizz past my eyes
Like tiny angels
Each one unique
Each one in disguise
Floating gently and aimlessly to the ground
No drama
No sound
Pure of spirit
Pure of sight
An amazing winter delight
Painting the world fresh and white
And tonight?
You hush the world to sleep
Falling steady and deep
Your silence a comfort
Your beauty to keep.

This Egg

There were a dozen eggs
Oval and smooth
Hard yet fragile
With a centre that at any time could ooze...
Out.

One by one you took each egg
Into your hand
Sometimes you squeezed slowly until you heard them crack apart
And sometimes you violently broke them with intent
Like you tried to break my spirit or break my heart.

One by one all were smashed and tidied up
Like it had never happened
Like nobody knew
That it was you.

The very last egg
You placed it in the centre of your hand
It was planned
Fingers closing softly all around
This one would hardly make a sound
As its very soul poured along the ground
All the life draining away
Wasted before it had even begun
For your fun.

        You squeezed and you pressed
Adding more pressure, adding less
    Something just wasn't right
     This egg just held on tight.

This egg was me
And what you couldn't see
Is that you were finally foiled
Because this egg is hard boiled
You can't break me and just tidy up for a new egg and a new day
No way
This egg is here for justice,
This egg is here to stay
And nobody is tidying up, or putting me back in the box.

This is What it is

It cannot be contained.
How could that ever be?
It is in every orange sunset
That kisses you and me.

And at night
When we curl up tight
To shut out the cold
And keep out the light
It's those soft fresh sheets
And the soft heartbeat
That we hear
In our ears
To let us know
We are safe and we are alright.

It is in everything that we eat
That we enjoy
It's how we love that chocolate
Or that wine
And savour it until the very last bit
But we felt it!

And sometimes
It is in the silence
When we're at peace and still

      And we fill in the gaps
      And close our eyes until
      We see what we need
      We see who we need
      And there it is
      And we no longer need
      We have it...

In our hearts, in our heads, and in our lives
Parents, children, friends, husbands, wives
What disaster or pandemic can keep this thing away?
Can destroy a force, can ever keep LOVE at bay?
It might take lives, and hopes, and dreams, and so much more
But LOVE?
It can knock on love's door
But it will never be a guest.

We meet through windows, on zoom, and even Perspex screens
And through our masks we smile toothy smiles that no-one ever sees
Because we do it out of love, and it oozes out of every pore.
Because we are the guests allowed in, and through love's door

Waving washed and gloved hands aloft
Dropping off shopping for those who cannot
And calling those who need to speak

Who have seen no-one, for a whole week
That's what it means
Or so it seems.

It is feeling it, and doing it, and showing it
It is owning it, protecting it and nurturing it

> We may die
> But love never dies
> We love as we die
> We are loved after we die
> And THAT is the power of love
> It lives on with us
> And through us
> And because of us
> We are LOVE!

Mrs Brown's Bucket

She was the walking widower
Known throughout the town
The woman with the bucket
Poor eccentric Mrs Brown
Just a washed-up old tramp
A nothing, a clown.

But she was so much more than the eye could see
She was content with her lot, she was free
"What's in the bucket Mrs Brown?" they would call
Not a question but a taunt, and she ignored them all.

Until one day someone really did ask her why?
She had walked with her bucket all this time

"Some days I fill my bucket with love
And distribute it to those in need
Some sweets through the letterbox for the children who have none
Or a wave and a smile, for the man with bad knees.

Some days it's full of kindness, little notes I write with care
Dropping those voiceless words to those who feel there is no one there
Sometimes it's full of hope that things will be alright
Whilst other times when I need to, I choose to carry it at night.

I fill it full of all the rage and anger I hold inside
I fill it full of negative words they shout as they pass me by.
At night my bucket has a hole, so I can lose what weighs me down
So when I carry my bucket in the cold light of day
I can carry the hope, that I have for this town.

My bucket is always at least half full
Or sometimes it's filled to the brim
On the outside, it is just a bucket of course
But for those who believe, they receive what's within.

My bucket holds everything I could ever hold dear
All the priceless things, that I wish to share
My bucket is my key to happiness
It's the only way I know, how to show I am there.

So yes, I am the widower, Mrs Brown
And eccentric? I wear that with pride
But I'm far from washed-up, or poor, or a clown
I'm Mrs Brown with the bucket, and I know what's inside.

And today? It's full... of pride!"

One Day My Life Will Become Landfill

One day my life will become landfill
Tossed aside as if it had never been
All those years becoming nothingness
As if it were all just a dream.

One day my things will be cast aside
The ornaments and trinkets that I dust with love and care
Will become the next generations to share
And perhaps, for a while, some may be cherished and displayed
But sure enough, as time ticks by
And generations move on in the blink of an eye
All but the most precious of my trinkets will die
They will be tossed aside
Landfill!
And not one person will wonder why.

One day my brain may cease to work
And all my memories may go array, confused, berserk
And, I may not know the ones that I hold dear
Or may not truly see you, as you visit and keep me near
And all those moments we shared, where we laughed and lived
And all those dreams that we had, and hoped we'd fulfil
May mean nothing to me…

In the debris of my mind
In a life that could be unkind
It would simply cease to be
And even I, may not know me
And all that life and love,
Would seem... like landfill... for the soul.

One day, and hopefully only when I'm grey, and old, and ready
My body will become more frail, and more unsteady
Until eventually, my functions may cease to be
And all that would be left of me
Is my soul, and the memories I have left behind
For future generations to find
Like clues from a life that was,
That ceased simply because...
It was time... and that's what we do
Live life as best we are supposed to
Until we too, become Landfill.

And so today we are here,
Alive!
To make the most of life and strive
Not for the trinkets and possessions to share
With those, for whom, they'll hold no joy or care
But to fulfil the dreams that we have right now
And to enjoy those that we love and have around
To leave our mark in the world through our own happiness, joy, and fun.
To achieve all the dreams we dreamed, and to be someone.

So that when it ends, and all is said and done
And the night has fallen, and taken away the very last of the evening sun
Perhaps in hundreds, maybe thousands of years' time.
In the Landfill of a long lost internet file
Our face may smile to a generation far removed
Who may read of what we did and who we loved
And may take the time to learn about us and see
That although we are Landfill, and long ceased to be.
We lived, we loved, we laughed, we cried, we died
We cared about those whom we left behind
We wanted to leave a small mark on this earth
That could survive the landfill, through our own self-worth.

One day my life may become landfill indeed
Tossed aside as if it had never been
But remember, my life was filled with love and those I loved
And no Landfill could ever conceal a life well lived.

The Grand Opening

It was Monday, the grand opening of Aldi
The Mayor and his wife were the guests
Cutting the red ribbon with infectious glee
And putting a shopping trolley to the test.

Yes a mad dash around the food laden aisles
Grabbing all the best goodies to hand
Everything grabbed in two minutes
Would go to the local food bank.

Mrs Mayoress was a woman possessed
An octopus just couldn't compete
But Mr Mayor got all his chains in a twist
And tripped over his own two left feet.

Down he went with a squeal and a fart
His best trousers split at the seams
His soiled Mr Blobby underpants
Keeping his Crown Jewels discrete.

He grabbed at the Mayoress in an attempt to get up
And her lovely silk dress tore in two
Out popped the twins in a snip of a bra
And out popped her bare buttocks too.

A scuffle ensued with a tangle of limbs
And profanities thrown in for good measure
The look on the face of the young homeless man
Was one of huge disbelief and great pleasure.

"On behalf of the food bank I would just like to say
Thank you to the Mayor and Mayoress
The meat and two veg with the fat chipolata
Was not a meal we expected I profess.

But the huge rump of beef will be a real treat
Best served rare as we can all see
I've never seen a Mayoress with so much to offer
With a buy one, get the other rump free."

And so it was that the Mayor and the Mayoress
Went home just a little upset
But the homeless man had his fill in more ways than one
And the grand opening had been one of the best.

Have Hope

Have hope
For hope is the friend that will find you when you are adrift and lost
Have hope
For hope will be the hands that catch you when you fall. It will hold you aloft
Have hope
For hope is the light that will shine on you, to guide you when all is dark
Just have hope
For hope is the strength that will sustain you when you are weak and ready to disembark...
From life itself.

For without hope what are we?
What fear would eat us up?
If hope was never in our cup
That we could drink aplenty
What nightmares would crush us whilst awake?
If hope was not ours to have, and hold, and take.

And remember...
No one can steal our hope
It is a gift we receive and share
In a world where we owe it to ourselves to care

No disaster can suppress or quash our desire
To save and be saved
To love and be loved
To have hope and give hope
That burning fire
That lives inside us all
To let us know
We can survive
We can thrive
We can be the person we need to be
So that when it seems that all is lost
And we have nothing else to give
We can give hope.

For even in the darkness, we can still see
Even through hatred, we can learn to love
Even through war, we can find peace
And even on the worst of days, we can hope to see a better day
There is always a way!

So today
In a world where so many have lost so much
Where others seek to destroy and erase the hope, that is our crutch
Be strong!
Hold your hope like a beacon
Be the friend, the hands, the light and the strength
Be brave
Be hope
And never forget to have hope.

My Forever...

I held you as though it were the first time
Tender and shy
I felt you melt as if it were the last time
Your heart beating against mine
You didn't know
My wish to never let go
Not wanting to show
This was my memory of the last time.

You were so fragile
Skin and bone
As I held you firm and gentle
You were "home" to me
I felt safe
And I wanted that for you
I am so grateful that you never knew
But somehow, I did
And I was afraid I would miss the last time
So this last time... was mine

As I rubbed your aching bones
I smelt you long and deep
I wanted to keep
Your smell of hot buttered toast
And Sunday roasts
And all the things you did so selflessly
That sometimes we failed to see
I wish I could tell you now.

And even when it got awkward
And you tried to escape my embrace
I greedily held you in place
My small piece of forever
That I endeavoured
Would stay with me... even when you could not
I knew that when you walked... away
It would feel like you had slipped... away
And my heart cracked a little at what was to come
When it was all undone.

And so,
We let go
And in the silence of a noisy room
In the solitude, and all too soon
The moment had passed
And in my heart so had you
I just knew
And I didn't say
But that day
That day is... and will always be
My forever.

Cut the Power

It was intensely dark and cold
Tensions were high
Suspicious of every noise
Each solitary person passing by
The question on those trembling lips
"Why?"

Throughout the bleak grey days
And those long dark nights
Relentless!
No end in sight
No light
Where once
In years gone by
It had been bright.

As people whisper in corners
Or murmur in chastened tones
The ever-growing fear
And the ever-present drone.

There has been no power for so long
A temporary cut, or so they said
But winter yielded all it had to take
The victims, weak, were waxen, cold and dead
And on your head
They said.

For every vote
For every bank note
That left this country
Surrounded by this murky moat
Of darkness
Of which there seems no end
No sympathy to lend
Time to defend.

It's not the power cuts
And it's not the dark
It's the power that we need to cut
The contrast, stark
The interest inflator
The guileless partaker
The rampant dictator
Elected by oppression
Creating dark depression.

It's not the power cut for hour after hour
Oh no!
Stand up
Be brave
It's time to cut the power!

Fade Away

So, I saw you fade away
You chose your own elegant, graceful way
The conversations about you changed in form
No longer jovial, pain relief now the norm
I saw you hide the truth and I played along
Although, I knew that pretending was entirely wrong
I should have shared all our lovely memories of you, with you
And talked of all the things I loved that you would do
Instead, I watched you hold yourself upright
Talking politely, and then, slipping out of sight
And I watched all those close to you look so scared
And I watched, but didn't react, because I cared
For you needed to live this life of duplicity
To show us all, the old you, in its simplicity
For fading was not the person that you were
Living, was the life you chose to share.

My Clock

I think I've got a defective clock
OMG sometimes time passes so bloody slowly it's almost stopped
I tap it
I shake it
I will it… just move on
And then in a moment it speeds up and that thought is completely gone.

    Then time passes so quickly as if in a dream
        Busy, busy, busy, never serene
           And before you know it
         Another Monday came and went
        Another week, month, year, spent
           And where did it go?
            I really don't know
              Tick, tick, tock
           That funny old Clock
          In a frenzy and flurry
           All in such a hurry.

And then my body clock joins in, going crazy and awry
It doesn't know the correct bloody time of day
I didn't get the batteries
And I dropped it on the floor
Until it's stopped and even that, doesn't work anymore

Then a pause
The menopause
Which of course you cannot pause
Like time itself.

Then just when time is ticking on nicely
True to the second precisely
Life throws a bloody curveball straight at the clock
As painful as a kick in the cock
And time bloody stops for a while
Or at least truly stood still for someone you love
As it plucks them to reside up above
And just like the old grandfather's clock itself
It all just stops
And you think… never to go again
But then like you, it restarts and chimes
Because even when the world falls apart, you cannot stop time
Only time… eventually… will stop you

So now I just listen to the clock…
When it appears slow I don't will it ahead
I enjoy those little stolen moments instead
When it goes fast I work quickly to find a way
To slow it down just a bit and eke out the day
When it pauses or stops
I acknowledge why
I take the time out it allows me
To heal, then I try
To restart the clock
And to keep in good time
For time waits for no man
And time… is always… on time.

For the Love of...

"Oh for the love of God!"
I hear them laugh again
And I know who they're talking to
It's always the same
One word..." Betty"
And as far as I can see
She's labelled the new one
So what does that make me?
If she is new,
Then does that make me old?
If I am the quiet one
Then is Betty bold?
If Betty is labelled "naughty"
Then is my label "good"?
And has Betty been labelled greedy?
Because she eats all my food?
Of course I am the brown one
Whilst Betty is the red
Betty is much taller
But I've got the bigger head
But really what does it matter?
We both love just the same
Betty and Delilah
Those are both our names
And we run and we play
And we eat and we sleep
We get out all our toys
And get under their feet
But we love them
And lick them
And snuggle them up

Because they are our human parents
And we are their pups
And whatever our labels
My favourite of all
Is when they call us their babies
And say, after all
That whatever the labels
That others may say
To them we are perfect
And we're here to stay
So perhaps over time
Their exclamation might be
"For the love of dogs!"...
Of course, that's Betty and me!

Forever and Always

I am alone!
In the silence I see you,
Eyes shut tight, and warm water slides away
Salty on their way... to nowhere.

I feel the loss heavy weighted on my chest
Catching deep in my throat
And in this salty moat
I am frozen! Screaming silently
As I run away... to you... but to nowhere.

And the tide is out, and you are so far away
Just a small dot on a horizon
That leads to nowhere, and everywhere
But I swear, you are there,

Yet as grains of sand sift swiftly through my fingers
Carelessly slipping and falling
There is no stalling... time.

I cannot hold you, or hold back the tide
It comes as it always will, in a wave that engulfs me, and smothers me
In the saltiness I cannot see
You... or me.

Drowning, and you hold me
I rise,
Eyes open, then I see
I am alone!
You are not here,
It is just me.

Warm water slides away, salty on their way
But I will not drown, when I fall... down
I will close my eyes tight, and you give me sight
Of you... like a dream
Silently I scream,

For in the silence, I see you
That sweet pain,
Every grain,
Of forever... spent,
Falling silently and gently to the ground.

I could not catch you, as you caught me
I could hold you, as you held me
I could not save you, as you save me
I can only dream... and you exist in my dream.

Eyes shut tight, and I am alone
But In the silence I see you
Forever I love you
And I swear,
When I need you, you are there
Forever and always.

Wish List - Be a Lover

I wish everyone would think before they speak
And whatever words they wish to say
In whichever way
They soften it from Richter scale ten to Richter scale two
So put some thought into all you say, and all you do.

    I wish everyone would practise the word sorry
      If it's too hard... start off with the word lorry
        But stick with it. It's a great word to know
          So after a row, just before you go
            Although it sounds absurd
              Please use the "S"word
                It means a lot.

I wish everyone would remember to say "I love you"
We know we all do
So why keep it in?
Be proud, make a din
And scream "I love you, I love you, I love you"
Choose to be a lover not a hater
Sooner rather than later
While we still can.

I wish everyone would understand that anger comes from hurt
Let's be honest, we're all scrabbling around in the dirt
Thinking we're not good enough
We are!
So don't let anger or insults get too far
Don't attack to defend
Let's not pretend
We are ALL hurt.

And let's not forget we are all in "life" school
No one is too cool to learn a thing or two
But the best lesson ever learned, was to be kind
Kindness will save us all… and all mankind
So don't sweat the small stuff and shout
Breathe, and let only kindness out
Today we can do all these things just to please
Because tomorrow is never guaranteed.

So, from me…
"Lorry,
I'm sorry,
I love you,
I'm proud of you,
You are always far more than good enough
You're perfect
…as any human can be
Today is the first day of forever
You'll see.

So, let's all be kind
Be a lover
Let's save all mankind".

A Walk on the Dark Side

When the darkness encompasses you with its icy grasp
And you are rendered all but blind
When you hear nothing but your raspy breath
As it whispers deep, and hollow into the night.

When you feel you might have died
Yet your heart beats just the same
When the emptiness swallows you whole
And the nothingness comes to claim...
You.

When you walk along the dark side
And you have swallowed all the blame
In this cruel game
Just stop.

For even when you have nothing, then you still have time
And in that pause, prepare to climb
Out.

For in that moment where it seems that all escapes are barred
When you have painstakingly followed every route but never got too far
Then fear not.

Time will always bring along a new moment
And a new day to greet
Time will restart the heart that is often too scared to beat
Time will allow your ears to hear the blood as it rushes through your head
Consciously reminding you, you exist, you are not dead.

    Time can heal life's wounds
  And be the friend that can be kind
    To realise that you are not blind.

  Urging you to dare to step ahead
 And decide where you should tread
 To be brave enough to open your eyes

And when you see the glint of light
That glistens like hope through the canopy of trees
Get up off your knees
And stand tall
You have walked on the dark side
But discovered the light after all.

Listen as the world whispers wistfully in the air
You are right there
Alive... Journey on.

To be Valent

At a glance there was no chink In his armour
Nothing to alarm her
That inside was soft and runny
Sweet to taste as golden honey
She did not know at the time
That this was his ine
To be gallant
To be nothing but valent
A victory away from everything and nothing.

She was young and free
Some might say a hippy
Her heart firmly on her sleeve
Ready to leave
For when she would carelessly and selflessly
Give it away
Until bruised and battered
And relentlessly tattered
It would return to its brave soul
Barely whole
A beat away from everything and nothing.

It was 2015
She was barely nineteen
And he in his 20th year
And knowing nothing of love
Both looked up above
And wished their special someone was here.

It was Friday 13th
Not the best day they say
And yet for some it was a night like no other
For when midnight struck
Two little arrows were stuck
Into the hearts of two most unlikely lovers.

So on that Saturday morn
Jogging just after dawn
On the 14th of February that year
As she fell to the ground
He barely made a sound
As he caught her and held her heart near.

He had first met her at nine
And had spun her a line
That Spider-Man had nothing on him
Then they met at fifteen
She a stroppy teen
Breathing in so he'd think she was thin.

Now as she fell to the floor
It mattered no more
To hold pretences of heroes or waifs
Carefully lifting his sleeve
He mopped up her tears
And off slid his heart in her way.

Her eyes met his gaze
And she knew through the haze
This kind man will always be mine

She had fallen in love
Heard his words from above
As he whispered "Be my sweet Valent... ine!"

The Weekly Shop

I went to the supermarket today
I bought one bag of get a grip
Two tubs of ice cream
One pot of let it all out
Three packets of you scream I scream
Two bags of potatoes
And one pouch of patience
One tin of red tomatoes
One scourer to remove complacence
Three buckets of I told you so
Two dozen eggs
One sponge to get egg off your face
And a huge pack of pegs
One washing line to air the laundry
Two loaves of bread
A pot of Vic menthol
To clear the head
A blister pack of sarcasm
And a tube of antiseptic
Three packs of paracetamol
I wanted five, but the till wouldn't let it
A twenty-four pack of toilet roll
To mop up all the shit
A pack of hold it altogether
And an emergency sewing kit
Four pints of full fat milk
And a three pack of large knickers
A fridge magnet that says "looking good"
And a multi pack of snickers
A family pack of mixed up nuts

And eight tins of Heinz baked beans
A toilet duck and an air freshener
And a pot of Vaseline
I bought glasses and molasses
And a new set of plates
A crate of ambition
And a tray of never too late
Five huge rip off shopping bags
To carry my haul
And I brought a suitcase of cash
To pay for it all
And when the checkout lady noted
There was an offer especially for me
An offer of don't fuck up this week
On a buy one jar get one jar free
I smiled as I solemnly asked her
What the refund policy is on don't shout
And as she checked with the manager
I opened my pot of let it all out.

GOLDEN

A golden light
Warm and bright
Illuminating where darkness falls
Squeezing tight to halt the fall
For all
The father, mother, brother, sister, friend
From inception, until the end
Ever being, ever seeing, everlasting, ever there
To care
The arms that even on the coldest of nights
Hold on tight
Generous and selfless
Aching arms, to push us to the light
Until a new day
And we pray
Free.

> The peace to stop the noise
> The grace and poise
> The dignity
> The beat of our hearts
> That we hear
> In our ear
> And when it beats in fear
> Always near
> To slow that beating heart
> Until we start
> Ourselves... to beat again.

The noise to stop the very peace
That can deafen some
Until you come
Singing gently, a lullaby
Floating high
Like a dream
To halt the scream
We are never alone.

The hope that binds us
That even when we are powerless
And cannot understand
We are brave enough to take a stand
To do what is right
And never lose sight
We can prevail.

The one who woke us up
And mapped the path to journey on
Making choices as we go along
The guide to lead the way
For a new day.

And in the end, where the beginning may well
proceed to start
As we all depart
We know we will be home
As we have always been, home
Basking in the light
Unconditionally.

Never losing sight
All this time
The gift that we unwrapped
And used every day
Never fades away
And though it may sometimes dim
Until it is as black as night
We grip with all our might
To hold on tight
For that golden light
Just basking in the glory of the day
Golden.

The Masterpiece

We are dying from the moment we are born
But too busy living to see
But time... as time always does
Will make history out of you and me
You'll see!

We are like a piece of art
And as we begin life, and earnestly start
The very structure begins to exist
Until the brushstrokes persist
To produce a masterpiece
Each one unique
And ready for critique
Which will surely come.

Some will never be admired or desired
Others will be weathered and worn through
But even the most beautifully adorned
Cannot escape the truth
That one day they will expire
Reaching their finest hour
And just when they peak
And perfection is within reach
When the picture is all but perfect
It will all be washed away
In the storm to end all days.

The colours will fade and blur
And the outlines melt away
Until one day
The canvas will be bare
The white space denying what was there
But every piece of art
Has played their part
In the masterpiece of existence itself
And that portrait of self
Was you.

Creaking Doors

Surrounded by tragic endings and new beginnings
Chapters that open and close
Layered by screams and laughter
Mingled with despair and hope.

    So much more than creaking doors
        And pointless wars
        And keeping scores.
    So much less than Sunday best
        And being impressed
        Or being blessed.
        Just guided chances
    And fleeting dances with destiny
        Each day refreshed.

    And yet... for what and for whom?
        There is no cocoon
        Just a chance to fly
Where wings can expanse the entire world
        Or wither and fail.

Not all will soar
Some destined to fail from the start?
Others destined to begin the moment they fail and fall.

    But... the playing field will tilt and turn
        The tide will ebb and flow
        Time will surely pass you by
        Chances come and go.

But the grasp?
Sometimes of an iron will,
Will, hang on until the end
As the precipice will hang like doom itself
And only oneself
Can decide if fate and destiny
Will stand testimony
Or if there is more
Behind creaking doors to explore...
And soar.

I had Waited for this Moment for so Long

Eyes wide open
Why so dim?
Picture Perfect
And yet closing... outside in
Distortion, no sense of proportion
Of now, or what was to become.

Darkness, falling fast all around
Then that moment that would shatter the ground
Where you walked
Where we walked
Where we hoped to walk again
The moment in time that stood still.

And suspended
We float
In nothingness.

And all this time silent
Like a sniper taking aim
Suddenly and violently upping its game
Until Darkness came to claim
And it would never be the same.

"Oh, what a shame" they would say
Just a rumour? "A tumour?"
"If only they'd known sooner".

Eyes wide open, diminished
Finished!
Whilst today, took all our yesterdays
And although tomorrow was secure
No-one could be sure... of
Who you would be, or are.

And you?
You knew nothing at all
Like time itself had been erased
And only this moment was real, existed, or had ever existed at all
Every moment passed... Stolen!
And tomorrow would be stolen too... For you
Just another day, passing through
Erased!
On repeat
Delete!

Childhood to adulthood grew
We held fast and knew
One day tomorrow would come
And finally reclaim the chance to become yesterday
When finally, our yesterdays would return to you
As we would too
And although you may not see as you once could see
You would see us,
And you would see me.

       Eyes wide open
And through the darkness you see
       And I stand aloft
         Suspended
          I float
  Bathing in nothing but hope.

I had waited for this moment for so long
Thinking you were gone
And all that time, you were searching through
To find all our yesterdays for you
And this moment is finally true
And for this moment, with all my heart, I thank you.

Autumn

I am in Autumn
The tree is creaking in the breeze
The leaves are tired and ready to fall
Asleep!
Just for a while
Until the warm sun replenishes the life,
The smile.

I want to enjoy my Autumn
I don't want storms and silent moments
I want golden light and laughter
I don't want hustle and bustle
I want ambles and rambles
I want happy ever after
Even if it's just a made-up thing
Thought up by those, still in spring.

I want to live my Autumn my way
I don't want to spend my Winter rueing the day.

Whilst my creaky tree-like limbs still bend and arch
And my leaves still hang on for the bright green
shoots against the muddy brown bark
I will do my salutation to the sun
I want to commend myself for a job well done.

I surrendered to you my long hot summer
Enjoyed every day
I would not wish to change a moment.
But now I say
Autumn is here,
And ploughing through at breakneck speed
And I don't want it to supersede me.

Winter will be cold, I'm sure
And my limbs will droop and wilt
So autumn must be special
In Autumn I must replenish… be rebuilt
This is my Autumn
My season to shine
And for that I feel no guilt.

Autumn is here, and so am I.

Hiding Tenaciously from the World

Weighed down by life
She clambered around
With body armour, life vest
Goggles, and ear buds to block all sound.

Hiding tenaciously from the world
Concealed, yet obvious in plain sight
Heavy, cumbersome and burdened
Gripping on surreptitiously with all of her might
To survive those too bright days
And those torn velvet nights
Unseen, unnoticed, unimportant
Forgotten and surpassed
Cruelly cast aside
Destined to hide
Away.

She thought he could not see
But he saw her.
She gestured "Me?"
Removing the goggles to be visually free
Her barrier down
He softly spoke
She was awoke.

She read his lips
And as he nuzzled slowly in
She removed those deafening earbuds
She allowed his voice within
And so he melted her with his smooth hot chocolate tone
And his earthy guttural moan
Of ecstasy
As they slumped to the ground... as one
Her life vest discarded
He wouldn't let her drown
And with body armour swiftly removed
She succumbed.

>High on life
>She danced around
>Eyes wide open
>Ears to the ground
>Light, safe and free.

Every Picture

They say every picture tells a story
And that may well be true
But our story, paints a picture
Our story starts with you.

Your eyes that shine like sapphires
Placed the blue up in the sky
The colour of summer cornflowers
Streaked with the palest grey of a cloud passing by.

Your skin the colour of honey
Paints the tiniest grains of sand
Where we lie in the dunes on a hot July day
As I caress your skin, and you hold my hands.

Your lips as red as cherries
As we pluck them from the trees
And teeth as white as the crest of a wave
As you buoy me up on stormy seas.

Your hair the yellow of the brightest of suns
Dazzles my eyes until I cannot see
That dusk has fallen, and the darkness reveals
How the stars light the picture that tells our story.

Every brush stroke, another day
Every water colour, a day of rain
Every shade a vibrant hue
Our picture tells a story
And now our story is me and you.

The Very Essence of Who I Used to Be

My head says it cannot be me
Yet before me I see, the very essence of who I used to be
As if all those precious years had slipped away
To a forgotten, dusty, distant yesterday
And just in the very corner of my eye
I believe the lie, for a while
And I dream.

The smile is just the same
As laughter trickles through the parted cherry lips
Eyes alive,
Dancing,
With the lithest set of honey tanned limbs, and curvy swinging hips
Youth, eternalised in time
Yet the reflection is not mine
It is not a mirror stood in front of me
Just a perfect vision
An escape to what I used to be.

There is no dam to hold back the years
We cannot determine how kind time will be
But certainly
Time as it always will, withers and decays
Subtlety each day
Until outwardly we become someone else
As if somewhere we lost oneself.

I look back at you, as if peeling back the years
You look towards me and they all just disappear
And melt away
Those precious days.

And yet I'm sure from the corner of your eye
You see how all those years have passed me by
And how in twenty, thirty, forty years to come
You too will review the damage those many years
have done.

To you my image of what I used to be
Enjoy those youthful years, for in time you might
also only see
The very essence of who you used to be
In you, I see me.

It's Your Loss

Carpe diem, seize the day
For yesterday has in essence, breathed, then all but passed away
Merely a memory
Intangible, and beyond imaginable, for some.

And if the day carelessly tumbled, endlessly from your grasp
Shattering into myriads of pieces of splintered glass
Alas…
Sadly, it was your loss, and your cross to bear
It was your day.

Tomorrow is simply a gift that we might never receive
Undelivered or returned
Unearned.

But today is present, placed lovingly in the palm of your hand
Undetermined, undefined, willing you to understand
The infinite and illimitable opportunity this day proffers.

For those who will befriend and court fate
Today is never too late.

Today we can be the self that we choose
Saunter or dance, down our own path, in our worn comfy shoes
We can love endlessly, give generously, help selflessly
And live graciously.

For when dusk slowly descends, and gently falls to the ground
And all around the vivid colours fade, and melt, to grey
When the silence holds you sweetly, tightly, and contentedly in its grasp
And there is nothing left, no words that dance, that find your lips for you to say
Then you will fold away… to sleep awhile
Creased and crumpled, surrendered in your slumber
To gloriously and torturously reflect and wonder
At all our yesterdays that we visited, and held for just a while.

Those days not seized?
Regrettable
But never forgettable
For it is those days that will catch, and burn, like fire in your throat
Take your breath, as they float… away

A squandered, unconquered, abandoned day
A huge price left unspent, yet unpaid
And the price tag in the smallest print will simply say
It's your loss.

Song for Blake

For all the times that we listen
To the same old songs
With the same old words
And we sing along
And all the times, that we drive
In the car for miles
Going everywhere and nowhere
Just to see your smiles
But what else would I do?
I'd sing a hundred songs,
And drive the whole World around for you.

> For you were meant to be
> Brought into this World
> Especially for me
> And you have stolen
> Each and every part
> Of my ever-breaking heart.

For all those milestones that they said
You would never reach
Well, who would have known,
That you would find your feet?
And for all the times that you struggled
Just to find the words
But "I love you Mammy" were the ones
That made all the others blurred
So, what else can I say?
I love you more each day.

For you were meant to be
Brought into this World
Especially for me
And you have stolen
Each and every part
Of my ever-breaking heart.

For all the pain that you've been through
In your small, young life
And the wonderful people
Helping you through strife
And all the times when quitting
May have felt so right
But then the strength you brought
Made all that darkness light
And so, what else can I do?
I will always fight for you.

For you were meant to be
Brought into this World
Especially for me
And you have stolen
Each and every part
Of my ever-breaking heart.

And I am not alone
I have you
And where I go
You go too
And you are not alone
You have me
And for all time
That's just how it's going to be.

For you were meant to be
Brought into this World
Especially for me
And you have stolen
Each and every part
Of my ever-breaking heart.

For all those cheeky little smiles
Where your dimples show
And the frustration you feel
When you are ready to blow
And all those moments of pure joy
Just for you
When you laugh out loud
At the wonder of something new
So, what else would I do?
But show the World to you.

For you were meant to be
Brought into this World
Especially for me
And you have stolen
Each and every part
Of my ever-breaking heart

For all the times that we listen
To the same old songs
As we drive along
Well, what else would I do?
I'd write this song for you
What else would I do?
Sing those words "I love you"
Well, what else would I do?
I'd write this song for you
What else would I do?
Sing those words "I love you".

About the Author

Katherine has always lived in the South Wales Valleys, inspired by its contradictory barren and beautiful landscapes. She is happily married with two children, and two huge poodles. She has been published in *Poetry Wales*, and has also been published as part of a charity Poetry anthology. Her love of Poetry can be attributed to her inspirational and unforgettable English teacher Mr Alex McAleer who brought the world of words to life. She has ironically worked in the world of numbers and statistics for thirty years but has returned to her passion and love for verse and rhyme in more recent times. This is Katherine's first collection of published poetry.

Printed in Great Britain
by Amazon